CW00486836

EMBER

www.chellebliss.com

CHELLE BLISS

USA TODAY BESTSELLING AUTHOR

Carrie Ann Ryan, Corinne Michaels,
and Jessica Prince (when she was awake)

Thank you for the months of laughs and 'shit' talk.

It was also nice to have an audience for my morning
naps...sometimes a girl just needs to close her eyes to
create something beautiful.

Without your friendship and pestering this book
would've never been finished.

I love you three assholes.

MEN OF INKED: HEATWAVE SERIES

Book 1 - Flame
Book 2 - Burn
Book 3 - Wildfire
Book 4 - Blaze
Book 5 - Ignite
Book 6 - Spark
Book 7 - Ember
Book 8 - Singe
…and more hotness to come.

To learn more,
please visit *menofinked.com/heatwave*

Do you LOVE audiobooks?

LISTEN TO AUDIOBOOK SERIES NOW

Flame is now available in audiobook.
Visit *menofinked.com/heatwave* for more info.

Get a Text Audio Alert
Text **AUDIO** to **24587**
USA Only

EMBER COPYRIGHT © 2021

Publisher © Bliss Ink April 20th 2021
Edited by Lisa A. Hollett
Proofread by Read By Rose
Cover Design © Chelle Bliss
Cover Photo © James Critchley

Chelle Bliss
MENOFINKED.COM

PROLOGUE

ROCCO

THERE'S NOTHING PEACEFUL ABOUT DYING.

Not for the person taking their last breath.

Not for the person there as witness.

Not for the people left behind.

And yet, the world doesn't stop moving for a single second to mourn their passing. There's no universal pause for the life that's been extinguished. One minute, they are alive, and the next, they're gone.

I had a romanticized version of dying before that day. I never thought it was as brutal as the reality.

I was naïve, stupid, and young.

It was my youth that made me delusional, but that day...that very moment Carrie took her last breath, I was left with the reality that those whom I loved would die someday, along with myself.

I'd forever be haunted by the sounds of the life being choked out of her. Eternally traumatized by the way she pleaded for my help with nothing except her eyes.

I was powerless to save her. Unable to do anything except comfort her. I made a promise to myself after her body finally stilled.

I'll never allow myself to fall in love, opening my heart to someone so wide that they have the ability to destroy me from the inside out.

There was no guarantee of growing old, even though my family had seemed blessed with years well beyond the norm.

I knew every second that passed was another moment I was closer to the end. That simple fact stayed rooted in my mind for years.

I'd live life to the fullest, never tying myself down to something that could destroy me. I'd enjoy every moment, savoring new experiences. I'd lose myself in the opposite sex, forgoing emotional relationships and indulging in carnal pleasures instead.

At least, that *was* my goal, and I had every intention of keeping the promise I'd made to myself.

But then, she happened...

The one who had the power to destroy me if given half a chance.

The only person who made me believe the wonders of loving someone could outweigh the pain of losing them.

The one who changed everything.

And for the first time, the one I couldn't walk away from.

REBEL

"REBEL," HE WHISPERS, REPEATING MY NAME.

My belly flutters, something it rarely does. His voice is deep and caresses my skin as it washes over me.

I tip my head back, peering up at him, and the air catches in the back of my throat when I lock eyes with him. His gaze is so intense, I feel as if he's looking deep into my soul.

"You look like a Rebel, sugar." He smirks.

My knees go weak, but I keep myself upright by planting my hand firmly on the hood of my pickup truck. I suck in a breath, trying to fill my lungs.

The man is beautiful.

No.

He's more than that.

He's a work of art, clearly molded from someone's vision of the perfect male specimen.

Wide shoulders.

Thick biceps.

Big strong hands.

And a face that could make panties hit the floor with one single glance and very little effort.

I bite my lip, grounding myself with the twinge of pain, and remind myself he's only a man. A hot one, but still...just a man.

"Baby, I'm more like trouble than a rebel," I reply, somehow keeping the quaver out of my voice.

His smirk grows, exposing a dimple in his cheek.

Yep, a dimple.

Dimples are my weakness and not just those on the face.

The back ones, the two right above the ass...fuuuuuuck. I'm a goner for those every time.

"You two play nice," my best friend Carrie says as she takes her guy's hand, following him toward the cabin with the biggest shit-eating grin on her face.

I'm not sure if I want to give her the finger or blow her kisses for hooking me up with her man's twin brother.

She's been talking about this weekend for days. I didn't understand it until this moment. There were thousands of men on campus we could've partied with, but she said no one compared to the Caldo twins. I figured she was full of shit, but standing here, staring at one of them... She was not wrong.

Carrie gives me a wink across the yard before Carmello yanks her inside, no doubt in a race to get her naked.

"Whatcha wanna do, Reb?" Rocco's gaze is still firmly planted on me as if nothing else matters.

"I…uh."

Shit.

What I really want to do is climb him like a tree, removing the thin clothing from his body to see what lies underneath and explore.

But damn it, I don't want to be too easy.

A man should earn what I have to give, and I have no doubt Rocco Caldo is up to the challenge.

He doesn't take it upon himself to fill the awkward silence I create with the pause at his question. He stands there, studying me with those sinful eyes and smirking as I gawk at him, trying to remember simple words.

"Swimming," I blurt.

What the hell is wrong with me?

Swimming…what in the actual fuck?

Of all the shit to do in the world, all I manage to say is that lame answer. I've never had trouble talking to men before, but suddenly I've gone completely stupid in the presence of this one.

Rocco crosses his arms over his wide chest, his biceps bulging underneath the sleeves of his T-shirt like it is about to tear into shreds. And God, I want it to rip, giving me a full view of what lies underneath.

"You want to go swimming?" He tilts his head, eyebrows high, no doubt making some silent judgment about me that's way off base.

I shrug. "You're hot," I blurt out again, my mouth

working faster than my mind. I wince and slap my hand over my mouth.

Kill me now.

He laughs, and his eyes sparkle in the late-afternoon sunlight hanging over our heads.

"Fuck," I hiss, shaking my head and mentally backhanding myself for such a stupid mistake.

I've been in his orbit for all of five minutes, and every single thing that's come out of my mouth has sounded moronic.

"I meant *it's* hot."

"Uh-huh," he mutters, and that freaking dimple only gets deeper, drawing me in.

"I swear to God, I meant it's hot outside. You're just okay," I lie, but I keep on rolling through my ramble. "And between your black T-shirt and the sunshine, I'm sure you're hot too. Not hot as in sexy, but hot as in sweaty."

I just keep digging the dumb-ass ditch deeper. I should just throw myself in, cover myself with dirt, and call it a day. However cool I wanted to come off to the hot guy with the rockin' body, I have totally missed the mark.

Epic failure.

"You wanna feel if I'm sweaty?" he asks, his eyes dancing with so much mischief, I know he's all kinds of bad.

The kind that'll make my toes curl, but still filled with trouble.

"No," I snap, but fuck...I *so* do.

And I hate sweat. That shit grosses me out more than anything. I'd knee a guy before I'd let him get his arms around me covered in his own perspiration. It most definitely is not my thing.

He tilts his head, running his tongue along his bottom lip.

My gaze drops, following the path, wishing he were running that softness across my body instead of his own.

"You got a suit?" he asks, but I don't take my eyes off his mouth.

I can't. His lips are too plump and beautiful, ripe for kissing and made for pleasure.

"Um." I glance toward the truck, regretting blurting out swimming and the way I just stared at his mouth. "No."

"Bra and panties?"

I blink, and I part my lips. "Excuse me?"

"Are you wearing a bra and panties?"

I tip my head down like I somehow need the visual confirmation before opening my mouth. "Yep. Totally wearing them."

"Too bad," he whispers.

I snap my head up, eyes on him, taking in his smirk and a freaking dimple. "What?"

"Nothing." He reaches out and grabs my hand.

The contact sends a zap down my arm, through my body, and straight to the very spot that's throbbed since I laid eyes on the cocky hunk.

"What are you doing?" I ask, digging my heels into

the gravel underneath my feet and trying to make myself unmovable.

He gives my arm another light tug, and my body betrays me, moving with him. "To the back."

"The back?" I ask and peer over his shoulder to the field. "The backyard?"

"To the pond, sugar."

My eyes widen. "No. No. No," I say, drawing out each one a little longer than the last.

He laughs and takes another step, and again, my body moves with him. "It's safe. I promise nothing will happen to you. Well…" He smiles, stealing my breath again. "At least, nothing *bad* will happen to you."

My belly flips as my feet slide across the gravel, my body wanting to believe him even if my mind doesn't. "This is the South," I explain the obvious.

He doesn't stop walking as he peers over his shoulder at me. "And?"

"I don't know if you're new here or just dense, but there're gators in the water."

"You have a better chance of being bitten by a snake," he replies, like I'm the crazy one.

I swallow, and I don't even need a mirror to know all the blood's drained from my face. "Are you trying to talk me into or out of swimming in the pond with you? Because right now, you aren't making a good case."

Rocco stops suddenly and turns, but my feet don't get the memo.

I crash right into his chest with my face. I stagger

back, bouncing off his body like I'm a tennis ball slamming against a brick wall.

His hands are instantly on my upper arms, catching me before I have a chance to go down.

I gasp from the contact and the way his hands feel wrapped around my arms, holding me tight with his long, thick fingers. My body sways forward, and his hands tighten, sending tingles everywhere.

And I mean *everywhere*.

His brown eyes are locked on me, and so are his hands. He doesn't even let me go after I find my footing. "You okay?" he asks, his voice deep and sultry.

My mouth opens and closes, but nothing comes out. I'm too fixated on his brown eyes and the flecks of gold dotting the outer edges. "Fine," I squeak and tense when his thumbs stroke the tender skin on the inside of my biceps.

Those same honey-brown eyes sweep over my face. "Don't see any damage."

"Damage?" I whisper.

"Your face is still pretty even after colliding with all this."

I can't stop the smile from coming to my lips. "All this?" I raise an eyebrow, staring back at him.

"It's a lot of man to hit for such a small and pretty face."

"You did not just say that," I tell him, biting my lip to hold in my laughter. "Tell me you did not just say that."

CHELLE BLISS

His hands finally fall away, but the heat from his touch stays imprinted on my skin. "Tell me I'm wrong."

"Fine. Fine. You're a lot of man, but honey, I'm a whole lotta woman, and running into a man like you and bouncing off without a scratch is my superpower," I say, finally finding my inner Rebel instead of the weird, silent girl who crawled out of the truck a few minutes ago.

He crosses his arms again, tilting his head at the same time, a move he seems to have perfected. "Is that a challenge?" The muscles in his arms flex at the same time his lips twitch, and goddamn it, my eyes go right to them. "'Cause I love a good challenge."

I take a step forward, closing the space between us, and roll up onto my tiptoes. "You've been playing in the minor leagues, baby. I'm the pros. I've been with college men while you've been kissing high school girls under the bleachers, learning how to satisfy pussy and failing."

His face doesn't change at all when he says, "Rebel, sugar, I'm going to rock your world. You can bet your pretty ass on that."

"Are you even eighteen? I mean—" I pull back, looking him up and down. I know he's of age and could pass for a much older guy without a shadow of a doubt, but it doesn't stop me from saying, "I don't want to end up in jail, even if you're the one chasing me."

He laughs, tipping his head back, the sun glinting off his white teeth. "I'm nineteen, sugar, but I totally dig you're a cougar."

I narrow my eyes on his happy, hot-as-fuck face. "I'm twenty, which hardly makes me a cougar."

"I'm younger. Therefore, you are, in fact, a cougar. And, babe..." He pauses, licking his thick, pink lips. "Given half a chance, I'm going to make your weekend unforgettable. You're going to be ruined and will never look twice at the other college men again without remembering what it felt like to have me between your legs."

I chuckle, but fuck, my belly flips, and I have to resist the urge to squeeze my thighs together. "You think you're that good?"

I'm playing with fire.

I know I am.

The man's looks alone could make any girl bend over and beg for cock. And yet, here I am, tempting him with all the right words, wanting his lips on mine and that hard, hot body crushing me into the sheets.

His eyes drop to my mouth when he says, "I know I am."

Rocco Caldo is an absolutely cocky, arrogant, beautiful asshole.

I slide back, needing out of his personal space and a chance to catch my bearings. I have to come up with a way to make myself not appear to be so easy and to give myself an out.

Younger guys usually kiss like shit. Sloppy, wet, and way too much tongue. It is the only thing that pops into my mind as I stand there, him staring at me and my body vibrating from all the energy flowing between us.

"If you can sweep me off my feet with one single kiss, I'll think about giving you a little more. But—" I hold up a finger "—if you fail at this one task, we're going to binge-watch romance movies all weekend while we listen to those two bang each other's brains out. Deal?"

Rocco's smile widens as he lifts one hand to his chin, running his index finger across his bottom lip. "And if I give you the kiss of a lifetime, I get you any way I want you, all weekend long. I mean, it's a win-win for you because you're going to have so many orgasms, you're not even going to remember your name, and it's a win-win for me because I will too."

"Honey, you're nineteen. You're not a miracle worker. I can get myself off if need be. You've just got to get me close."

He shakes his head slowly, his eyes dancing. "I may be young, but I know my way around the female body, Rebel. I promise you that."

"Oh. Okay," I tease and nod. "Whatever lies you need to tell yourself to protect your—"

His hand comes out, grips the back of my neck, and hauls me forward so fast, I barely have time to brace myself for impact. My chest doesn't even touch his before Rocco's lips are on mine, consuming every ounce of me.

Holy moly.

He moves me as if I weigh nothing, and I immediately turn into a pile of horny goo right there in his grip.

Before I can catch my bearings, his other hand meets the one already on me, cupping my face.

He kisses me harder, taking my mouth wet and fast, along with my breath.

I tilt my head, opening my mouth, giving him everything I have and wanting him to take it. My knees wobble, but I stay standing because he's holding me to his body, my face in his hands, keeping me that way.

He pulls away and I think the kiss is over, but he stares at me for a second, our mouths barely touching, and I see it.

The lust.

The want.

The need.

It burns bright, and the look is unmistakable.

I stare back, the same feelings no doubt showing in my eyes as we soak each other in.

Before I can process the craziness of the situation, his lips come back down on mine, crushing and brutal but so freaking sexy, my entire body tingles and lights up.

Rocco doesn't kiss like a boy.

No. No.

He manhandles me in the perfect way that would make any girl beg for more, and I'm not immune.

He talks a big game, but he has the moves and the lips to back up every single promising word.

And I know one thing—I want more.

My arm snakes around his shoulders, gripping on to him in case he tries to let me go. I fear if he did, I would crumple to the ground at his feet, nothing but a pile of hormones.

Damn. I hate that he was right. I hate that I've wanted him from the moment I saw him, but now… now, I want him even more.

Everything falls away as he kisses me, possessing my mouth. All the animals moving through the forest around the cabin seem to vanish. The sun is no longer blinding as he gives me shelter with his body. But the heat never wanes, only intensifying as it comes off him in waves, permeating my body.

He doesn't let up or let go, his hands only tightening around my face but still somehow gentle. There is no escape, no respite, no moving out of his orbit, as I have been captured from the moment his lips hit mine.

I know then, as he pulls away and I am left panting… Rocco Caldo will be more trouble than I bargained for.

2

ROCCO

CARMELLO BANGS ON THE BEDROOM DOOR, NOT understanding boundaries. "You two done in there?"

"No," Rebel moans as I double down on my efforts to make her come again.

My face is planted between her legs. Her fingers are tangled in my hair. She holds me there like I am going to go somewhere, which I'm not, even if the place burns down around us.

"A little bit more. Just a little bit…" she breathes, coming out as almost a whisper.

She arches her back as her thighs clamp down around my head, and her fingers pull at my hair, lifting it from the scalp.

The chick is mint. And when I say mint, I mean fucking mint.

She's sassy as hell with a bangin'-ass body that would drive any man insane. Her sexual appetite rivals mine, and in the last twenty-four hours, we've barely left the bedroom.

I don't care that I can't breathe with my face buried in her pussy, suffocating the life out of me.

Her moans grow louder the harder I suck. She bucks, nearly convulsing through the orgasm, pussy contracting around my fingers like a vise.

Hell yeah, baby, you like that.

I love a woman who voices her pleasure, letting me know when I hit all the right spots.

The other chicks I've been with have always been so quiet, more worried about being embarrassed than letting me know where and how they need to be pleased.

But that isn't Rebel.

She's loud as fuck.

She doesn't know how to be quiet in the sack, and if a man has failed to get her off in the past or the future, he is a fucking moron and can't take a cue to save his life.

She could have blown the windows out of the room when I pounded into her so hard I thought I'd thrown my hip out of joint. But nothing will stop me until she is left a quivering mess.

"Boy," my ass.

She discounted my skills and abilities because of my age, thinking I was too young to please her greedy pussy.

I want her to remember me for the rest of her life. Every man who touches her afterward will be compared to me even if she won't admit those words to my face. My goal is to ruin her and leave a lasting memory.

I lift my face from between her thighs as soon as her legs fall away, collapsing against the mattress like the rest of her body.

"Jesus," she mutters, resting her hand over her very naked and ample breasts. "I need to catch my breath."

I smile, staring up the length of her, loving all the dips and swells of her female body. She is exquisite in the low light, her skin covered with a layer of sweat only an orgasm can cause.

"Another?" I ask, my fingers still buried deep inside her, feeling every aftershock rock her core.

"No. No," she rasps, swallowing and squeezing her eyes shut. "I couldn't."

"Sugar, you could. I'd make sure of it."

Rebel lifts up on her elbows and gawks at me, breathing fast. "Who are you?"

"Your biggest fantasy." I waggle my eyebrows, smiling at her.

She shakes her head, her cheeks pink. "Or my biggest mistake."

I raise an eyebrow and start to move my fingers ever so slightly, pulling them out and pushing them back in, careful to rub against her G-spot. "The best mistake of your life, Reb. Any other man ever made your toes curl like that?"

She tips her face upward toward the ceiling, exposing her throat, and she moans, bearing down on my fingers.

I don't care what comes out of her mouth or how much she wants to deny what we have, the chemistry between us. I know she wants me, and even after this weekend, she won't have her fill.

I keep working her, two fingers inside until she's fucking my hand, driving herself back up and doing nothing to alleviate the wood I'm sporting.

I can't walk out of this room until I've buried my cock deep inside her, letting out all my pent-up energy so I won't be walking funny all night.

She hisses as I pull out my fingers, leaving her wanting and empty. But I rectify the situation quickly, grabbing her by the ankles and flipping her over in one swift move.

I find her waist with my hands, hoisting her hips in the air and giving me the most beautiful view and perfect angle.

She turns her head, gazing at me over her shoulder as I run one hand down her spine and over the swell of her ass.

"Fuck me," she whispers, panting, full of need. "Hard, baby. I want it *hard*."

My cock jerks, liking her words and sick of waiting. I reach over, grabbing a condom, and tear it open with my teeth.

She watches me.

"Tell me you love my cock." I roll the latex over the head and down my shaft, staring at her. "Tell me how much you want it."

Rebel's not shy, and there's nothing demure about

her. Without hesitation, she says, "I want your cock, baby. All of it, buried inside my pussy."

The mouth on her sends electric shocks through my body, practically short-circuiting my entire system.

With my hand wrapped around my dick, I inch forward, lining up the tip to the very spot that's brought me hours of pleasure already.

"Not slow. Don't take me slow." She licks her lips as she stares down her back, hands planted in the mattress, back rigid and straight. "Hard and fast. Fuck me like I've never been fucked before."

I bite my lip, holding in the moan crawling up my throat, threatening to break free before I have a chance to sink into her soft heat.

I move my hands to her hips, pulling them higher, and when our bodies are lined up, I thrust inside her, hard, deep, and unforgiving.

She gasps, and her ass rises as our bodies slam into each other. "Just like that," she says before turning her face back to the mattress and bowing her head like she's about to have a personal conversation with Jesus himself. But the only worshiping I'll allow her is that of my cock.

I pound into her, over and over again, taking her deeper until she's panting and fucking me back, grinding her ass against my body, covered in sweat and sweetness.

I tighten one hand against her waist as I slide the other one up her back, flattening my palm in the middle and pushing her shoulders down into the mattress. She

CHELLE BLISS

gasps again with the change of angle, allowing my cock to slip deeper, filling her completely.

Rebel mumbles, speaking in tongues as I shove my dick deep, fucking her as hard and as fast as I can.

Her body no longer moves underneath my grip. Her lips part, she falls silent, and she almost stops breathing.

Her pussy milks my cock, pulling me over the edge with her until my legs begin to shake.

She flattens against the mattress, and my body falls forward, collapsing onto her back.

I inhale, taking in the scent of her skin, trying to catch my breath as my legs struggle to recover.

Our bodies are stuck together at every point we're still connected. Our ragged breathing matches, both gasping for air, bodies heaving.

Absolute fucking perfection.

Another knock. "We're leaving in ten. Everyone's waiting for us if you two can come up for air long enough to leave the cabin," Carrie says with a slight giggle. "I told you they'd hit it off. They were made for each other."

They are both fucking annoying.

Neither understands personal boundaries, or maybe they don't care.

We never knocked on their door. Not once in the last twenty-four hours. They could've been dead in there, and it wouldn't have mattered. We were too busy doing our thing to worry about if they were doing theirs.

"Baby, they're not going to be walking down the aisle. Get that fairy tale right out of your head,"

Carmello replies from the hallway. "But from the sounds of it, that was one for the record books."

Claps fill the hallway, and I groan. "I give it a nine," Carrie states. "If he'd lasted a little longer, then it would've been a ten and worthy of a standing ovation. Just a wee bit short."

"What am I, baby? Am I your ten?" he asks her, but I already know what her answer is going to be, and so does he.

They're gross. Almost too sweet and perfect with their cutesy names and the bullshit they say to each other.

"You're a twenty, darlin'," is his response.

"They're gross," Rebel echoes underneath me, her voice still raspy and hoarse.

I roll over, bringing her with me to face the ceiling. I find her waist with my hand, feeling at home there like we've done this a million times before. "You want to go with them?"

She peers up at me, her head on my shoulder, tucked against my body with her ice-blue eyes on mine. "I think my pussy needs a break."

"So, is that a yes or no?"

"They have food and beer at this party?" she asks me, running her black fingernails down the middle of my chest. "Because I could use a refuel for later." She giggles, probably thinking I'm spent for the night.

But she has no idea who she's messing with, and I'm no chump. I can fuck all night, and I am about to prove that to her for the second night in a row.

Sure, we'd fall asleep for a short time, and I'd wake her up with my mouth or fingers between her legs, causing her to moan.

I smile, liking her way of thinking. "Then let's go, sugar. Eat and drink all the things because later, I'm going to need my fill again."

She blinks, tongue darting out, running across her lip. "I'm not going to be able to walk when I leave here tomorrow night."

My smile only grows wider, and I press my lips to hers, pulling back to whisper, "I want your body to remember me forever, Rebel."

She swallows, her blue eyes pinned to my brown. "I don't think that's going to be a problem."

And with those words, I give her one long, hard kiss like I did when I won her over in front of the cabin, before rolling away.

"Aren't you going to shower?" she asks, leaning across the bed, watching me grab my jeans off the floor. She's checking out my ass. Her eyes are hungry, and I like the look on her.

I shake my head, taking the condom off before stepping into one leg. "I'm not washing you away, baby. I want to smell you on my skin all night. Not ready to let you go that fast."

She gawks at me, her eyes dipping to my dick as I tuck my length into my jeans and zip them up. "Whatever you say, big guy," she whispers.

"You love my cock, don't you?"

"No." She looks down, fumbling with the rumpled sheet.

I reach down, touching my fingers to her chin, forcing her eyes back to my face. "Don't lie."

"It's nice," she teases.

"Kittens are nice, Rebel. My cock is a beast and a freaking work of art."

She stares me straight in the eyes, a small smile playing on her lips. "You think really highly of yourself."

I raise an eyebrow, not breaking eye contact. "How many times did my cock make you come?"

"A few," she mutters, averting her gaze.

"Lying doesn't become you," I whisper against her lips as she leans forward, going for another kiss.

I pull away, leaving her wanting more and loving every second of teasing her.

"You're an asshole."

I grab my T-shirt off the floor where she'd thrown it and yank it over my chest, smoothing it down with one hand. "You wouldn't want me any other way, would you?"

She grunts, pulls herself up, and climbs off the edge of the bed. "Maybe," she says, sauntering past me slowly, swaying her hips and that fine ass to drive me crazy.

And it works too.

I'm a goner for this chick.

Twenty-four hours and I'm ruined.

I keep teasing her, but I'm the one who's fucked. There is pussy, and then there is *pussy.* Rebel has the second. The unforgettable kind that crawls into a man's soul, making him a different breed and always thirsting for more.

"I'm going to make you admit it before tomorrow," I tell her.

She turns her head, peering over her shoulder, a wicked grin on her face. "I look forward to it," she whispers before closing the bathroom door so slowly I strain to see her body for every last second before it disappears.

Fuck.

I could seriously fall for this crazy-ass chick I didn't even know yesterday.

Going to this party is the smartest thing to do.

I need a break before she takes me under, ruining me more than I could ever ruin her.

3

REBEL

TWENTY MINUTES LATER, I STEP OUT ONTO THE FRONT porch with Rocco right behind me. I don't need to turn around to know how close he is; I can feel his presence.

Carmello has his ass planted on the hood of his car, and Carrie is between his legs, laughing as he kisses her neck, whispering something—no doubt dirty—to her.

Fucking Caldo twins.

They are wicked.

No men should be as hot as they are.

And Rocco's ability to use every inch of his body—his mouth, fingers, cock, and tongue—to bring me pleasure should be absolutely criminal.

"Why you walkin' so slow, Reb?" he whispers in my ear, his body heat licking at my back.

I glance over my shoulder. My mouth is so close to his, I have to force myself not to touch my lips to his. "I'm not in any hurry, Roc."

His lips almost touch the corners of his eyes. "Sore, sugar?"

"No," I lie, trying to walk normally, but goddamn, my pussy feels like it's been through the wringer.

The moment his hand touches the small of my back, propelling me forward, I suck in a breath and somehow don't wobble and fall on my ass.

It's a goddamn miracle too.

"Finally." Carrie raises her head from snuggling with her very own Caldo. "Didn't think you two were ever going to be ready to leave the bedroom."

I stare at her, telling her all the things without telling her all the things. "I needed some fresh air."

"Uh-huh," she says, giggling. "By the way you're walking, I think your lady parts are battered and bruised."

"Shut it," I tell her with a glare.

Carmello slides off the hood, keeping his hands planted on Carrie's hips. "Ready to roll? Everyone's probably already there."

"Where are we going?" I ask Rocco.

"The locals have a party in the woods." Rocco opens the back door for me to get in with one hand, ushering me that way with the other. "It's perfect for a night like this, unless you want to stay back and…" He waggles his eyebrows.

I fall backward, avoiding him tempting me back inside. "Party sounds great," I tell him, pulling my legs inside and settling into the seat, resting my weight on one leg to give my middle a rest.

Rocco folds his body inside and places his hand on my thigh, sliding me across the seat with ease.

"What are you doing?"

"Sitting with my girl." He smiles, snuggling up next to me and throwing his arm around my shoulder.

I slide out from underneath his weight, move to the other side of the car, and grab the seat belt, fastening myself tight. "No, you are not. I can't sit in the middle. It's dangerous."

"Fine," he tells me, moving over to where I am, pinning me to my door before strapping himself in with the flimsy middle seat belt. "This works too." And again, he throws that heavy limb over the back of my seat, resting his hand on my shoulder, tangling his fingers in my hair. "Good?"

"You're relentless," I whisper, gazing up at him through my eyelashes.

He angles his face closer. "Rebel, sugar, if I weren't, you wouldn't have had ten orgasms today. So, let's not play games or tell untruths. My relentlessness has been more of a bonus for you than me. Now, get those lips over here and give me a kiss."

I glare at him, trying to pretend I'm pissed, but sitting this close to him feels right. His brown, honey-flecked eyes are trained on me, and all I can see are those thick lips that sent me over the edge so many times I lost count. "No," I snap. "I get a break. And when I say break, I mean break. Ten minutes. No lips." I turn my face forward, crossing my arms over my chest, trying to make my body rigid.

He slides his thumb across the sensitive skin near my ear where it meets my jaw. "You sure about that?"

My pussy convulses because the dirty whore living between my legs clearly hasn't been sedated. "Five minutes," I plead, feeling my resolve slipping. "Just five."

What the hell is wrong with me? Can't I resist this man? Damn it.

I've never been so attracted to someone so quickly. And then there is the chemistry, which is un-fucking-believably off the charts and makes completely no sense.

Carrie and Carmello get into the car sometime during the exchange, and she slides over to the middle, wrapping her arm around her man like Rocco did with me.

She is purring in his ear as he fires up the engine, tearing out of the gravel driveway and spinning the tires.

I stare straight ahead, trying to keep my eyes off the hot piece of ass next to me. Plus, I am trying to stop myself from thinking about all the pleasure he gave me earlier and has promised to deliver again later.

Instead of seeing the road pass by, all I can see is Carrie as she nibbles on Carmello's neck, giving no shits who is watching.

"Carrie, seat belt, babe," Carmello tells her, but doing nothing to push her away.

"No," she whines, moving her hand to the back of his head and sinking her teeth into his neck.

He moans, giving up the seat belt fight pretty

fucking quick. I can't see her other hand, but I am pretty fucking sure it is somewhere in his lap, probably stroking his cock through the tight-ass blue jeans he has on.

Rocco takes my hand in his, lifting it to his lips, rolling his tongue around the tips of my fingers.

I close my eyes, knowing the battle isn't winnable, and right as I am about to cave, the car jerks to the right.

My eyes fly open.

A scream tears through my throat as Rocco's right arm slams into my chest, pinning me to the back seat.

Oh God.

Oh no.

No. No. No.

The tires screech as Carmello swerves, and Carrie's scream matches my own, only louder.

Please don't let this be happening.

"Fuck," Carmello hisses as the car jerks again, going the opposite direction from the first time.

All I see is the line of trees heading our way. All I feel is Rocco pinning me to the seat. All I hear is the yelling and the deafening squeal of the tires.

But before I can brace myself, everything goes black.

4

ROCCO

MY BODY JERKS, AND MY EYES SNAP OPEN.

Reality hits me a few seconds later.

I blink, trying to clear the haze from my vision. Something heavy is in my lap. I bend my neck, seeing it's not a something, but a someone.

Carrie.

Her body is bent over the front seat, her head resting against my legs. Her back is clearly broken. No one is meant to twist that way, not even the most flexible human being.

"Carrie," I whisper, lifting my fingers to her face.

She gurgles a response. Blood oozes from her mouth, spilling onto my jeans, and making it impossible for me to understand her words.

My eyes flicker to the right, finding Rebel with her head resting against the window of the car. Blood is dripping from her chin, plopping onto her T-shirt and seeping into the material.

I grab her wrist, pressing two fingers below her palm, looking for a pulse. I exhale when I find it, strong and steady, beating normally.

"Mello!" I yell.

He doesn't move.

No one does.

Carrie and I are the only ones awake, and in this moment, we're totally alone.

"Stay with me, baby. Don't talk," I beg her as she struggles to breathe. "Help's coming."

But none is.

The road near the cabin is as empty as it always is. No one will find us for hours out here in the middle of nowhere.

"Mel!" I yell again, lifting my hand from Carrie's face and placing it on his shoulder, giving him a shake.

He stirs, not speaking right away. As he blinks, his eyes soak in the reality, despite the air bag blocking most of his view.

"What the..." he says as his voice drops to a whisper when he turns his head, noticing Carrie's body not where it was a few moments ago.

"Call 9-1-1, brother. Call fast."

"Is she alive?" he asks, lifting his ass and retrieving his phone from his back pocket.

"She is," I whisper, going back to softly brushing my fingertips over her forehead, soothing her.

But she won't be alive for long. That much I know. Not with the amount of blood she's losing and her inability to breathe.

The ambulance is useless, but I don't want her to know that or my brother.

"Make the call, Mel," I tell him, keeping my voice low and even for Carrie's sake. "This is so fucked up," I mutter to myself, wishing I could make everything different.

I am powerless and helpless, knowing she'll die in my arms.

Mello's on the phone, talking to someone and rambling about what happened.

Tears are streaming down the sides of Carrie's face as she stares up at me with her green eyes.

She says something, words I can't make out but wish I could.

"Shh, baby. Don't talk." I continue stroking her face as gently as possible, hoping she knows I'm here. "Just stay with me. You're going to be okay," I lie.

Our eyes are locked, saying all the things that can possibly be said in a moment like this without speaking a single word.

Fear.

Remorse.

Sadness.

Anger.

Worry.

Pain.

Terror.

Suddenly, her body stills, her eyes still fixed on mine but no longer filled with life.

Mello's girl has taken her last breath and died in my arms.

"Is she…" he says as the phone drops from his hand.

"Yeah, brother. She's gone."

His eyes widen, and the color drains from his face. "This is my fault. I killed her," he whispers.

"Mello, none of this is your fault."

He grabs his head, rocking back and forth. "I was driving. Oh my God. I killed her. I *killed* her."

"Stop," I demand, pinned by Carrie's body, unable to shake sense into him. "You can't control nature."

Fucking wildlife.

Three deer ran into the middle of the road, and Carmello swerved, trying to avoid hitting them but smashing into a tree instead.

No matter who had been behind the wheel, the outcome most likely would've been the same.

"Rebel?" he asks, his gaze moving to her body next to me.

I reach to my side, wrapping my fingers around her wrist to find her pulse again. "Alive," I breathe.

My fingers are still stroking Carrie's forehead. I know she isn't here and can't feel what I'm doing, but it doesn't matter.

I can't stop myself from repeating the movement over and over again until the faint sounds of sirens fill the air.

"Rocco?" Rebel whispers, finally coming to.

She'd been sedated. Too distraught to sit still and crying uncontrollably. The medical staff thought it would be in her best interest to keep her calm and still until they knew the extent of her injuries.

I lift my head from her bed, touching her hand, and I see her confusion. "Reb, you're okay, baby," I reassure her.

"What happened?" She tries to sit up and winces, collapsing back into the hard mattress. "Where's Carrie?"

My fingers tighten around hers, sweeping my thumb across the soft skin on top of her hand. "We were in an accident. There were deer, and Carmello swerved."

"Where's Carrie?" she asks again, but this time, there's more panic in her voice. She moves her gaze around frantically, searching for her friend, but there's no one here but us.

"She…" My voice drifts off, the words stuck in my throat.

Fuck. How do you tell someone their best friend died? I've never had to deliver that news. Never thought it was something I'd do at my age.

"She's what?" Her eyes widen, and she tries to move again.

I raise my other hand to her shoulder, guiding her back down to the bed. "Reb, she's gone, baby. She didn't make it. I'm sorry. So, so sorry," I whisper.

"Don't lie to me. Where is she?" Rebel asks, squirming underneath the pressure of my hand.

"Stop moving, Reb. You have some bruised ribs from the seat belt, and you messed up your wrist. The doctor said he'll be back in with the rest of your test results soon while we wait for your aunt to get here."

Rebel's eyes fill with tears as she stares at me, her gaze looking right through me. "She can't be gone. She can't be gone. She can't be gone."

"She is," I tell her, not knowing if I'm doing the right thing by telling her the truth.

She's already in physical pain, and now I'm adding mental anguish to the mix.

Her mouth opens and I think she's going to howl, but no sound comes out. Tears pour from her eyes as she cries in silence, the noise stuck in her throat.

I stand and insert myself into the bed, placing my arm on the pillow above her head. She curls into me, pressing her face into my chest.

I stay still, rubbing her back, letting her work through her grief and the sad reality that someone who was with us an hour ago is no longer breathing.

I haven't fully processed Carrie's death myself, and I am the one who watched her life drift away right in front of my eyes.

Rebel tips her head back, her water-filled blue eyes staring into mine, my T-shirt fisted in her palm. "Maybe they were able to bring her back. Maybe they…"

I shake my head. "They couldn't, honey." I stroke her hair, brushing it away from her damp cheeks. "She died in my arms. There was nothing anyone could do to save her."

I don't have the heart to tell her they didn't even try when they arrived on the scene. Carrie had been dead too long and had lost too much blood at that point for them to go above and beyond, trying to bring her back to life.

Rebel moves her face back against my chest, her body shaking with silent sobs as I rub her back, giving her time to grieve.

"I demand to see my sons." My mother's voice carries through the emergency room, and I immediately stiffen.

Izzy Caldo is intense on a good day, but knowing we were in an accident will no doubt take her to a whole new level.

"Carmello and Rocco," Ma says to someone. "Where are they?"

Rebel's too lost in her grief to notice my name, too busy sobbing against my chest, her limbs tangled around my body.

When my ma storms through the curtains, her mouth is open and she is about to say something until her eyes lock on me and then slide to the small woman curled in my arms.

"Hi," I mouth to her. "I'm fine."

Ma's shoulders slump forward in relief. "She okay?" she whispers, her chin dipping toward Rebel.

I give her a little shrug. "Not really."

"Hey, sweetie," Ma says in a soft and sweet tone, moving toward the other side of the bed. "You two okay?"

Rebel's sobs change, turning into a sniffle before her head comes up from my chest and she sees my mother. Her fingers tighten around my T-shirt again, but she does nothing to move out of my embrace.

"Rebel, this is my mother, Izzy," I tell her.

"Are you okay?" my mother repeats, not really reading the room. "What can I do?"

"Carrie's gone, Ma."

My mother's face pales. She knows Carrie. She met her a few times when she came to visit Mello.

They weren't exclusive, but they'd seen each other enough over the last year to be on my mother's radar.

"Carrie's gone," Rebel repeats my words before collapsing back against me, clinging to me like I am her lifeline.

My mother's frown is immediate and severe. I can only take the sadness of one woman at a time, and right now, I have to focus on Rebel.

"Go check on Carm, Ma. We're okay. I need a few more minutes with her."

Ma reaches out, placing a hand on Rebel's shoulder. "I'm so sorry, sweetie."

Rebel doesn't respond or shrug off my mother's touch. Her tears fall faster and harder than before as the reality of losing her friend seeps deeper into her soul.

"Can I do anything?" Ma asks us.

"I'd like to stay with Rebel until someone comes for her, Ma."

My mother only nods before finally leaving us alone.

Rebel peers up at me, and I glance down, meeting her sad blue eyes. "You can go. I'll be fine," she says flatly.

"No," I tell her, not moving or releasing my hold on her.

"Go, Rocco. I'm not your problem," she says through a sniffle and releases her grip on my T-shirt. "Go with your mother."

"No."

She shakes her head, pushing against my chest to get me gone. "Go. Just go. I want to be alone. I *need* to be alone," she begs.

"I refuse to leave you alone."

"Are you going to stay at my side forever?" she snaps.

"Sugar... Shut it."

"Fuck you. Right now, I want you to leave," she tells me, wiping the tears still flowing down her cheeks. "Please just go. Don't make me beg. Your family needs you."

"They can wait."

"Get the fuck out!" she hollers, hitting my chest as hard as she can with her one good hand.

I'm off the bed a second later, wanting her to be calm and knowing my presence isn't what she needs or wants anymore.

"I'm a big girl," she spits. "I can and always do take care of myself." She turns her back to me, curling into the fetal position.

I watch her for a moment, barely breathing, waiting to see if she changes her mind.

But she doesn't turn back around.

She doesn't call my name.

She does nothing.

I no longer exist, and she makes it perfectly clear.

I stalk out of the room a second later, and my mother is plastered at my side, checking me over like she did when I was a kid.

"Are you okay?" she asks in a rushed voice, placing her hand on my stomach as she guides me down the hallway.

"Physically I am, Ma, but mentally…"

"Your brother has a broken leg from the damn pedal. But you're going to feel like shit tomorrow, and so will he. Your mind will take longer to heal, baby."

She pulls me closer, snuggling into my side.

"Come on, baby, your dad's waiting for us. He took Mello to the car already. You two are staying with us tonight so I can keep an eye on you."

I'm not about to argue with her.

There is no point.

You can never win an argument with Izzy Caldo. I know that better than anyone.

"Whatever you want, Ma," I tell her, happy as hell to have a mother who cares so much about me and even happier to be alive.

"Ma."

She tips her head up and smiles. "Yeah, baby?"

"I'm never falling in love."

Her smile fades. "Never is a long time, Rocco. You'll feel differently tomorrow."

"I won't," I promise her.

She ignores my statement, muttering something under her breath as she walks me toward the car.

5

REBEL

Ten Years Later…

I peer up at the cabin, shielding my eyes from the afternoon sun, and push down the way my stomach twists with the memories.

Ten years have passed since I stood in this very spot, laughing in Rocco's arms as he nibbled on my neck. But then my world shifted, and in a blink of an eye, Carrie died.

I'd known tragedy before.

Hell, my entire life had been a train wreck. My father overdosed when I was in kindergarten, and my mother ran off soon after, preferring the feel of a needle in her arm to being a single mother.

My aunt got stuck with me since she was my only living relative. My mother left me on her doorstep with a note pinned to my T-shirt, taking off without ever looking back. There wasn't a day that passed afterward when my aunt didn't make it clear I was more of a burden than a blessing in her life.

She didn't have to remind me—although she did every damn day—because people can feel when they're unwanted…even at a young age.

My grades were good enough to earn me a full ride to college. After graduation, I didn't wait until August to head to campus like most teenagers. I left the first second I was allowed to enter my dorm, leaving my aunt and the toxic environment behind me.

That's where I met Carrie. She was the closest thing I had to family in my life. We had two years together, and in that time, we loved each other like sisters. The day she died, I truly became lost again.

I was destined to be alone.

Life had taught me that hard lesson.

Every time I loved someone, or they loved me, they didn't stick around very long.

It was my curse, and no one could tell me otherwise.

But for the first time, I was the one doing the leaving, and that put me in a bad way. Nearly broke, hauling ass for a better life, far away from the hands of a dangerous man.

The screen door swings open, and my eyes flicker to the very spot, hoping to see Carrie or Rocco, two people I've missed and never felt quite whole without.

"Rebel." Carmello, Carrie's old boyfriend, jogs down the front steps with a big smile hanging on his lips. "Damn, girl. You're lookin' good. Time's treated you well." He says those words as his gaze sweeps up and down my body, his body moving toward me, before finally landing on my face.

Carmello always was a flirt. Not the type of flirt that made a girl's skin crawl, but the kind that made a girl blush or swoon, depending on how thick he laid it on.

My face reddens as he moves closer, his eyes still sweeping over me as mine sweep down him.

He's filled out, grown up, no longer looking like the lean young kid I knew before. He is big, bulky, and freaking beautiful, just like his brother.

"You too," I tell him. "Not damn girl, but..." I swallow my stupid words before I embarrass myself more than I already have.

Not another word leaves my lips before he's in front of me, arms open, wrapping them around me like we've done this a million times before.

And it feels nice.

More than nice.

It feels freaking great.

My arms find their way around his waist as I hug him back, trying to ignore his rock-hard body pressed against me. "Thank you for this," I whisper.

The words aren't really adequate for the favor he is doing for me, but I give them anyway. He is saving my ass big-time.

Every place I called wanted first month, last month, and security deposit. Money I don't have or can't part with without leaving me penniless.

In a few more days, I probably would've had to call my aunt and beg for a roof over our head.

But then I remembered the cabin, hoping Carmello would rent it out to me without trying to steal the shirt off my back.

I could've called Rocco, but I'd done that in the past, and he'd never taken my calls. Carmello, on the other hand, picked up on the second ring and offered me a place to stay for a ridiculously low rate that fit my meager budget.

He tightens his arms around me as he brushes his lips over my cheek. "Don't mention it. Friends help friends, even ones they haven't seen in a decade."

Damn.

That was a low blow but totally justified.

My body stiffens in his embrace as guilt floods me. "I'm sorry," I whisper against his T-shirt. "I should've…"

"Don't," he says softly, splaying his hands across my back, the warmth of his touch burning hotter than the sun. "None of us were ready or able to—"

"I still don't know if I am," I say honestly, interrupting him before he can finish his thought. "And Rocco?"

Carmello pulls his head back, still holding me, until I can see his brown eyes, dotted with honey like his brother's. "He's…" A look passes over his face that tells me everything I need to know without him saying a word. "He's fine," he lies. "Doing great."

"Is he here?" I look over his shoulder, my eyes searching the porch and my stomach fluttering in anticipation of the possibility of seeing him again.

Please be here. Please. Please. Please.

Carmello shakes his head, peering down at the ground. "He had to work."

Damn.

"Oh." The butterflies vanish, replaced by a tightening knot deep in my belly. He doesn't want to see me, and that stings. "I understand. I was just hoping…" I stop speaking, not bothering with the rest of the statement.

Carmello moves his hand to his pocket, pausing. "Want me to call him and—"

"No," I reply quickly, shaking my head. "We're fine. Don't bother him."

Carmello's gaze focuses on my car, squinting. "We're fine?"

"My little girl is in the car." I motion toward the back seat where she's sleeping in her car seat, oblivious to everything and everyone around her. "Shit. I'm sorry. Our conversation was so fast, I forgot to tell you about her. I hope you're okay with her being here too."

He moves his hand to his neck before he takes a step forward, peeking through the window. "Damn, I didn't know you had a kid. That's so awesome." He smiles, looking at her for a beat before bringing his eyes back to me.

"Yeah." I rock back on my heels, looking at the ground. "She's five and completely exhausting."

"And the father?"

"Out of the picture," I tell him, dancing around the truth. He is out of the picture and very much dead, but

he isn't the man I'm running from. "I needed somewhere to get back on my feet, away from civilization,
and this place was the first one that came to mind."

Besides being close to broke, I want an escape.
Something far away from everything. Some place to get
lost while trying to put my life back together without
needing to look over my shoulder.

Carmello studies me, not speaking as his eyes flicker
back and forth between Adaline and me. "Things that
bad?"

"Not really." I tuck my hands into my pockets,
trying to stop myself from fidgeting. "As soon as I find
a job, I'll be out of here, so I won't take up the entire
rental season."

"There's no rush, Reb. Stay as long as you like. I'm
sure you want to spend some more time with your little
girl instead of hustling constantly. We don't rent the
cabin anymore, so we're not losing anything."

"You're sweet, Carm, but I don't have enough
money for an endless vacation."

"We don't want your money. Stay as long as you
like. Relax a little." Carmello gives me a tender smile.

Relax a little.

I haven't relaxed since college, and I'm not about to
start now. Relaxation is a luxury for those with money,
but besides being dead-ass broke, I am hiding.

"But I'll be honest, I'm not exactly comfortable
leaving you and her up here alone."

He is sweet for worrying, a trait I find admirable in

the Caldo men but have rarely encountered in other men I've met.

"We'll be fine. I've lived in the country before. I know how to take care of myself and my baby."

"This isn't the country, sweetheart. This is the middle of fucking nowhere."

"We'll make do."

He lifts up his hands. "Whatever you say. I'm just telling you how I feel, and how I feel is that this isn't safe or smart. Maybe I should stay for a few—"

"No. No. We'll be okay. You have a life to live, and we don't need babysitting." My nose tingles, and I push away the tears that I know are simmering just beneath the surface, ready to fall. "Thank you, though," I whisper, not trusting my voice to speak any louder.

He motions toward the car with a tip of his head. "What's her name?"

"Adaline." I turn toward my daughter, taking in her mess of dark-brown curls as she sleeps, and I smile.

She's the one good thing in my life.

No.

She's the best thing in my life.

Something I created that is beautiful and pure. The one person who won't leave me. I'll do anything to protect her, making sure she stays breathing and at my side.

"She's beautiful, just like her mama."

I blush and can't bring myself to look at him until the heat leaves my face. "There's nothing as important and wonderful as being a mother."

"I can't imagine the responsibility of raising another human—and to do it alone, too. You're an amazing woman, Rebel Bishop."

I give him a small smile, not feeling amazing in any way.

I've fucked up plenty in my thirty years on this earth.

I've had more bad than good, but Adaline is the best part of me and my life.

"The burden is heavy, but the rewards are great."

He's about to say something when his ass rings. He reaches back, fishing out his phone. "Hey," he says, holding up a finger to me before he walks away.

I take this as my cue to grab Adaline along with our bags, preparing to settle in for however long we're going to be here. But before I can open my trunk, a hand touches mine and gently pushes me away.

"I can do—"

Carmello shakes his head and ignores me. He grabs the two bags, phone tucked between his shoulder and his ear, and continues to talk to the person on the other end.

I stand there, watching his back as he heads toward the cabin, carrying the small number of things I have left to my name. He is one of the good guys, and he doesn't even try to be; he just is.

There's a muted squeal, and I'm quickly brought back to the reality in front of me. I'm not here to lust over a man for the simple reason that he carried my bags and has a fine backside.

I am here to live.

To survive.

To start anew.

"Hey, sleepyhead," I say, opening the car door to Adaline staring up at me with her big blue eyes.

"Mommy," she whispers, full of sweetness. She's in my arms a second later, resting on my hip with her head on my shoulder.

My gaze flickers upward as Carmello comes out of the cabin, the door slamming behind him. "Sorry about that," he says, not looking up until his boots touch the dirt at the bottom of the steps. He freezes as his eyes sweep over Adaline's sleepy face. "She okay?"

I nod. "She's just waking up," I reassure him, but I suddenly feel guilty about this whole thing. "It was wrong of me not to tell you about her. I hope you don't—"

He lifts his hand. "Rebel, you don't owe me any explanation."

"I'm sorry."

"Or an apology." He shakes his head, dropping his arm back to his side.

"Sorry," I repeat automatically, and I immediately cringe when he raises an eyebrow. "Fuck. It's habit."

Adaline gasps and stares at me with wide eyes, touching my cheek. "Bad word," she tells me.

The kid is like the gestapo when it comes to profanity. Something she picked up in day care.

Carmello laughs and continues toward us. "She's a cutie pie."

"She's totally irresistible." I roll my eyes, adjusting her against my side. "You're more than welcome to stay and babysit."

He stops his forward motion, almost recoiling. "While the offer sounds tempting, I have to get back to the city."

I can't stop myself from chuckling. *The city.* I know Carmello and Rocco's hometown, and nothing about it is even remotely city.

"Are you really going to be okay out here alone with her?" he asks again, clearly not confident in my abilities.

"Totally fine," I tell him before following him toward the cabin.

"I'll text you the number to the gun safe. Can't be too careful these days," he says like we're talking about the milk he might have left behind and not a cache of weapons.

"I don't think I'll need it."

I don't even know where I'd start. It has been years since I fired a weapon, way before I had Adaline. While some things are rote, my ability to be locked and loaded is not one of them.

He spins around to face me as soon as we're inside, his hand to his chest. "I'll feel better if I know you have access to everything here. There's no one for miles, and if you need to protect yourself or Adaline..." His eyes move to her, and his face softens. "You don't have to open it, but I want you to have the code. It'll put my mind at ease. Plus, there're bears up here."

52

Fuck. I'd forgotten why I hated Florida so much. There's always the possibility of wildlife lurking around every corner and crevice, ready to pounce and kill. Bear, gator, panther, and human…everything is a hunter.

"Okay. Okay. You can send it to me, but unless someone's busting down the door or a bear's trying to get inside, I won't be opening the safe."

"Thank you." He smiles, and my insides melt from the beauty of him.

Damn the Caldos and their good looks. They were able to land any girl they wanted, and from what Carrie had told me, the number was large back in the day. I have no doubts it is still the case, especially since he doesn't have a ring on his finger.

Not that I am looking, but…

I glance around instead of gawking at him. The cabin has been totally rehabbed on the inside, looking much different than it had when I was here before.

"Can I ask you something?"

"Sure." I adjust Adaline on my hip to get rid of my nervous energy from being this close to someone who reminds me so much of Rocco.

"Why are you really here?"

"I…" I pause, wondering how much I should tell him. I hate sharing my problems, and Beau is solely mine and no one else's. "I needed to start over. My life wasn't going how I wanted it to."

"How so?"

"How so what?"

"How was your life not going how you wanted?"

He's a nosy one, and normally, I'd tell him to mind his own goddamn business, but this is Carmello and he is doing me a favor.

I owe it to him, if no one else, to be at least a little open about my reality.

"Had a kid, got married, became unmarried, and then there was…"

His eyebrows furrow when I pause. "There was what?"

"Just a jerk I was dating. I cut ties and left before things got really bad, because he wasn't good for me or Addy."

He studies me and takes a step forward, closing the space between us. "How bad are we talking?"

"Pretty bad," I rasp.

His jaw ticks before he scrubs his fingers across his chin, staring at me. "Did he touch you?"

I peer down at Adaline as she fiddles with my hair. "I don't really want to…" I glance back in his direction, hoping he'll understand.

"I don't need all the details. I just want to know, did he *touch* you?"

The knot in my stomach tightens. The one that's always there, never uncoiling.

I hate talking about what happened, and saying the words out loud makes me feel like a bigger fool.

"Just one time."

"Fuck," Carmello hisses, tipping his face toward the ceiling.

"But I left right after. I wasn't going to raise Adaline

in a house like that, and I've never been anyone's door-mat. I'm not about to start now, no matter how hard life might be again without someone."

"Think he's looking for you?" he asks me.

I shrug. "I haven't given it much thought."

"When did you leave?"

"A few weeks ago," I answer honestly. "Moved around a lot, staying in a few hotels, but I had to settle somewhere because I was blowing through cash faster than I could afford."

Carmello starts to pace, his hands working against the coarse hair on his jawline. "Is he the type that would look for you?"

"Maybe," I say with a wince, hating to admit I ever let myself get tangled up with a guy like that. "I don't know."

The wood floors creak underneath his boots, but he doesn't stop moving. "You have your cell phone still? The one you had with him?"

"Of course."

"Give it to me." He holds out his hand and waits, his eyes hard, lips tight.

I blink, staring at his palm. "Why?"

"Did you pay for the phone, or did he?"

"He did."

"Fuck."

"Bad word," Adaline chides him without even looking his way.

I cover her mouth with my hand to stop her from saying anything more.

"Seriously, give me your phone," he demands, bringing his piercing dark eyes back to mine.

"Why?" I ask again, confused.

"Do you trust me?"

"I do."

"Then don't ask," he says like it's that damn simple.

One thing I don't do is trust easy. But Carrie thought highly of Carmello, and I trusted her more than anyone else in the world.

"Fine," I say, dropping my hand from Adaline's lips, and reach into my back pocket, grabbing my phone.

"Code?" he asks as soon as he has it in his hands.

"9-2-4-6."

He taps away on the screen, grunting to himself what I think is a slew of curse words, but I can't be sure with how low he's speaking.

I watch him as Adaline plays with my hair. She's been oblivious to the bad things around us. I've done my best to shield her from any hurt, something I never had done for me as a child. Although Beau, my ex, never held back from yelling at me in front of her, the one time he laid his hands on me, she wasn't in the room.

"Damn it," Carmello mutters in a low, growly whisper.

My eyes widen, and my feet move backward. "What?"

He doesn't respond before he grips my phone in both hands and snaps the sucker in two. I stare at him, my brain taking a minute to come to terms with what he's done.

I finally gasp, jerking my head back, shocked that he could do that, and that he did it without a second thought.

"Oh my God. Why would you do that?" I whisper, feeling tears starting to sting my eyes.

I've already started counting every dollar I have left to my name, and he takes it upon himself to break my phone without even asking.

It'll cost me a small fortune to replace it, too.

Money I can't afford to lose.

Money I don't really have.

"You can't stay here," is his only answer.

He says those words so calmly, I'm no longer angry about the phone but pissed at him for thinking he can tell me what to do.

"What?" I blink, trying to push away the tears before they have a chance to fall. "Why?"

"GPS, Rebel." He tosses my busted phone into the trash, kicking the cabinet door closed before stalking my way. "He probably already knows where you are. You can't stay here."

I don't move, but I keep my eyes on him as he walks toward my bags. "But..."

He bends down and grabs my things, ticking his head toward the door. "Come on. You can stay with me for a few days until we figure something out."

"We?" I whisper. "This is my problem."

"It's our problem now," he corrects me, his eyes

slicing to me as he stalks by with my bags in his hands. "You don't know if this guy will come after you, and if he does, what he'll do."

I follow him outside and stop on the porch, gawking at him as he throws my bags in his trunk. "What are you doing?" I ask, my mouth hanging open, Adaline still stuck on my hip.

"You can't take your car. Leave it here."

I'd laugh at his bossiness if the situation weren't so dire.

No phone. No car. Nothing except me and my little girl, along with a jerk who's trying to protect me but making things harder.

"I'm not leaving my car here," I argue. "First, you break my phone, something I can't easily replace. And now, you want me to ditch the only form of transportation I have. Are you freaking bananas?"

He slams the lid of the trunk and crosses his arms over his chest, giving me a super pissed-off and scary glare. "Did you check your car for a tracker?"

I blink again, gaping at him. A look I've had more than once in the last ten minutes. "A tracker?"

"Yeah, Reb. A tracker. You can buy one online and stick that shit under anyone's car and know where they are at all times."

Shit.

I hadn't even thought about that. My mind doesn't work that way. I thought I planned for everything, but I never thought about Beau tracking my phone or putting something under my car to keep tabs on me.

"People do that?" I whisper.

He tilts his head, staring me down, resting against the side of his car. "All. The. Fucking. Time."

"Bad word," Adaline pipes up, wagging her finger at the big guy who looks like he's about to blow a gasket.

"That's insane. Beau wouldn't..." I start, but the words die in my throat.

Would he?

He's texted me a few times, begging me to come back and promising he made a mistake.

It will never happen again.

I knew it was complete and utter bullshit.

Once a hitter, always a hitter.

Carmello stalks to my car, pulling the car seat out like it's something he's done a million times before. "Again, if he knew where you were, would he come for you?"

I swallow, feeling the knot in my stomach growing and festering. "I don't know...maybe." My voice rises on the last word.

"Then let's roll."

"But..." I don't move.

He shakes his head again. "In my car, Rebel. No arguments."

"Bossy asshole," I mutter as my feet touch the dirt path at the bottom of the steps.

And just as I open the door to his sleek red sports car, a truck pulls in and I freeze, catching sight of the familiar eyes I've never forgotten and have wanted to see for so long, staring right back at me.

6

ROCCO

My eyes lock on Rebel.

She stares back, her blue eyes wide, looking more beautiful than the last time I saw her.

I'm out of my truck before she has a chance to even think, stalking toward her. "What's happening?" My gaze moves from Rebel to my brother and then back to her. "Where are you going?"

I promised myself I wouldn't show up here, but no matter how hard I tried, I couldn't keep myself from coming. Too many things were left unsaid, and this is my only chance at changing that shit.

She hasn't moved and is barely breathing, and the dark-haired little girl in Rebel's arms is staring at me with the same wide eyes as the woman holding her.

Carmello lifts his hands, knowing I'm pissed. "Hold up," he says quickly, heading my way. "What are *you* doing here?"

I run my fingers through my hair, trying to calm

61

down—and failing. "You told me she was going to be here."

"You said you were busy," he reminds me.

"I got unbusy. Now, what the fuck is going on?"

He rolls his eyes and grunts. "Rebel's in trouble. She can't stay here, so I was going to take her home with me."

He's taking her home with him?

"Wanna say that again?" I ask, cocking my head.

I couldn't have heard him right.

Carm doesn't get involved in drama, and there isn't a woman outside our family he gives any shits about.

"She's in a bind, Roc. I figured I'd give her and the baby a safe place to stay."

"Not a baby," mini-Rebel says.

Rebel's blue eyes flicker to me for only the briefest of moments before they move back to my brother. "I'm fine here," she argues. "I don't want to go anywhere else. We aren't your problem or cross to bear. You two can go. Please…just go."

I've heard those words before and the last time I listened, but this time, that shit isn't going to fly.

If she is in trouble, I won't walk away like I did ten years ago, having regretted that decision ever since.

"Stay here," Carmello tells her, pointing to the ground where she's standing.

Rebel's face goes from pale to bright red at the way Carmello spoke. She opens her mouth to say something, but she quickly snaps it shut when the little girl in her arms pulls Rebel's face down to her level and whispers in her ear.

"What's going on?" I ask him, turning my back to Rebel and taking a few steps away from them with him.

He grabs my arm, moving me farther away and drops his voice. "She's running from an ex. She had her phone on and didn't turn off the GPS."

"Fucking dumb," I mutter.

"Yep. She has nowhere else to turn, so like I said before…I'm taking them home."

I stare at him, letting his words sink in. There is so much to unpack in that long-winded sentence. "Someone's after them?"

"She hasn't given me many details, but she's not in the mood to be found. I think that's why she wanted to stay at the cabin. We can't leave her out here alone, though, man. It's freaking desolate up here."

Anger bubbles in my veins, not only because Rebel's in trouble, but because Carmello didn't even think of me and how I'd feel about *him* bringing her home with him. "So, you were just going to take her home without calling me first?"

A small smile creeps across his lips. "Why would I call you about Rebel?"

My throat tightens, but I shake off the unfamiliar feeling climbing up my insides. "You know why."

"No," he says, shaking his head, smile still firmly planted on his lips. "Explain it to me."

I lift my chin, glaring at him. "Do we have time for this shit?"

"Not really, but I find it fascinating that you don't care about any chick, but you're territorial about this one."

"We have history," I remind him.

"You had a night."

While Carmello is technically right, we had way more than that. The words spoken and the soft touches we exchanged in those hours before and after the accident are things I can't shake. Hell, I've tried every day to get her out from under my skin and have failed miserably.

"We had more than that, and you know it," I growl, curling my fingers into fists at my sides.

"So, you want me to leave her here?"

"No," I snap, my fingers clenching tighter. "I'll take her."

He lifts an eyebrow. "And the kid?"

"Her too. They're not going with you. I'll take them with me. She and I need to talk, and I'll find out exactly what's going on."

"One night of being in her pussy ten years ago doesn't mean she's about to open up to you about her entire life, Rocco. It's been ten fucking years since she laid eyes on you."

I lean forward, getting into his space. "I know that, asshole, but she was mine and not yours."

He jerks back like I coldcocked him, but there's a smirk hanging from his lips. "She's yours?"

I close my eyes and sigh. "You know what I mean. Carrie was yours, and Rebel was mine."

"Was," he reiterates, dipping his chin.

"Whatever. I'm taking them," I tell my brother, pushing past him, and stalk toward her.

Her eyes widen for a moment as I move her way, and then her face softens. "Rocco," she whispers, backing up like I'm going to do something bad to her.

"Rebel," I say softly, trying to rid myself of the agitation my brother and the entire situation have stirred up inside me. "You're coming with me, sugar."

"Sugar?" she repeats on a whisper, wrinkling her nose. Her eyes move over my shoulder to Carmello, and I ready myself for what I know is going to come out of her mouth next. "I think it's best if I…"

"No," I tell her. "It's not best. You're getting in *my* truck and not his. We need to talk, and it can't wait any longer."

She lifts her chin, defiance in her deep-blue eyes. "Then maybe you should've answered the phone the numerous times I've called you in the last ten years."

Guilt floods me.

She's right.

I should've answered her calls, but I couldn't bring myself to hear her voice again…no matter how much I wanted to.

"I'm sorry."

"You should be," she throws back at me.

"Mommy," the little girl whispers.

Rebel glances down, shifting the little girl in her arms. "What, baby?"

"Be nice." The little girl smiles up at Rebel, blinking her big blue eyes, looking all innocent and sweet.

"I am, Adaline."

"No." Adaline places her tiny palms on Rebel's cheeks, moving her face closer. "You are not."

"I'll be nicer to the bossy man, sweetheart. I promise." Rebel peers up at me, cutting me with her blue eyes.

"We need to leave," Carmello says as he makes his way to his car. "I'll switch the car seat, and I'll drop your things off at Rocco's when we get back to town."

"No. Don't. We'll go with you," she tells him, completely going against my wishes, and starts to move in his direction. "I'd rather we go with you."

My arm shoots out, capturing her by the wrist and stopping her from taking another step. "Rebel, please," I beg, knowing we have words that need to be said, and if anyone can get her to open up, it's me.

Not him.

They have nothing together.

No shared history.

No connection other than Carrie.

Ours may have been short, but we still had something, and nothing or no one can change that. Not even the ten years we spent apart, not speaking to each other.

"Please just come with me."

Adaline makes a little kicking motion before pushing her way down her mother's body.

Rebel's eyes are fixed on mine before Adaline's feet

touch the ground. "Fine," Rebel says, but her tone is full of attitude. "We'll go with you."

Adaline moves toward Carmello and reaches for his hand, gazing up at him in that way kids do to steal your freaking heart. "I'm going in the pink car."

Carmello looks down at her in horror. "It's red, kid."

"Pink," she insists, pointing with her other hand to his souped-up red Challenger and holding his hand with the other.

"Red," he argues back, even though the fight is unwinnable.

He knows this, but my brother has never been one to back down from a fight, not even with a child.

"Adaline, you stay with Mommy," Rebel tells her, immediately turning away from me and striding toward her daughter and my brother.

"No," Adaline says. "Pink car, Mommy."

"Again, it's a *red* car." Carmello rolls his eyes with a huff before bringing his gaze back to Rebel. "Why don't you go with him, and I'll take her. We'll follow behind you two."

Rebel gawks at Carmello, betrayal in her eyes. "You're going to drive hours in a car with a five-year-old?"

Mello shrugs. "I do have younger cousins. I'm not allergic to kids, Rebel. Been around them my whole life. We'll be fine."

"She talks a lot. I mean a lot, a lot."

"So do most of the women I know," Carmello says, smiling down at the little girl. "She can keep me company while you two..." His voice drifts for a second as he looks across the yard at me. "...while you two get reacquainted."

Rebel peers over her shoulder at me, no smile on her face and only contempt in her eyes. "It's not a good idea."

"Go, Mommy," Adaline insists, pushing on Rebel's leg. "You go with the big man."

The little girl makes me smile. That's the thing about kids. Zero filter. It's refreshing to hear their type of honesty when they give exactly no shits about what they're saying.

Rebel kneels in front of her daughter and peers up at Carmello as he twirls his keys in his hand, standing near the hood of his car, before taking her daughter's tiny hands in hers. "You sure you're going to be okay without me?"

"Yes," the girl whispers, twisting her body like she's about to jump out of her own skin. "I'll be good."

Rebel sighs, giving her daughter a hug but looking only at Carmello. "She likes music. Just play it and play it loud, and she won't be an issue."

"Noted." He nods.

"Yippee!" the little squirt cheers before planting a big sloppy kiss on her mother's cheek. "Pink car!"

"It's red."

Adaline turns, lifting her arms and shaking them at Carmello. "Upsies," she says, instantly getting the reaction she wants out of him.

He plops her in the back seat, making quick work of the car seat restraints. "Let's roll, people."

"Let's roll," Adaline repeats, kicking her little feet, which are covered in hot-pink tennis shoes. "Bye, Mommy." Adaline waves with a big toothy grin.

Rebel stands there, not moving, and watches as Carmello closes the door. "You better drive safe and not like a race car driver with my kid in there."

"I have precious cargo." She stares at him until he ticks his chin in my direction. "Go," he tells her. "We're losing daylight."

"I didn't think things could get any worse, but clearly, I was wrong," she mutters as she stalks toward the passenger side of my SUV. "I'm not happy about this."

Those words are pointed at me as she climbs in, slamming the door as hard as she can to prove her point.

She's pissed.

Do I care? Fuck no.

We are going to talk.

She is going to tell me what we need to know to keep her safe. If she hates me for it, so be it, as long as she is safe.

I exchange a look with my brother. "This should be a great ride," I tell him while Rebel gives me the evil eye as she sits inside my SUV.

"Learn everything you can while the kid isn't around. Rebel didn't want to say much in front of her earlier, but she has no excuse now."

"Got it."

"And, Rocco," he says before I can grab the door handle and hit the road.

"Yeah?"

"Be nice to her and take it slow. Don't force her to talk."

My jaw ticks at his comment, and I grind my teeth, pissed. "I know, brother. I'm not an idiot."

"Debatable," he whispers as he opens the door and climbs inside to a squealing little girl.

I'm in the SUV a second later, and Rebel stares out the passenger side window, ignoring my presence.

I'll give her a few minutes to stew in her anger. She deserves the time to get herself situated after I forced her to come with me against her will. I wasn't trying to be an asshole, but she and I need to talk.

I let the silence fill the space as we pull out onto the road, with Carmello and Adaline right behind us.

We have three hours of road in front of us, and there is no way she'll stay silent the entire time.

Eventually she'll have something to say, even if it is only to tell me to fuck off, but that's when I'll have my opening, and I'll take it.

7

ROCCO

OVER TWO HOURS AND NOT A SINGLE SOUND FROM Rebel.

I was wrong when I thought she couldn't stay silent for the entire ride.

She could, and fuckin' A, she did.

Not even a sigh has come from her lips.

Nothing but complete silence and I am done waiting for her to make the first move.

"Rebel, we need to talk."

"About what?" she asks, not turning in my direction. "There's nothing to say."

"There's plenty to say."

"You didn't have enough to say to me when I called you before."

I grimace.

She's got me.

I did that. I'll own it.

My muscles tighten as she throws my past sins in

my face. "I said I was sorry. I should've picked up the phone. I wanted to, Rebel. I really did, but I just…" I grip the steering wheel tighter as I glance over, getting the back of her head. "I just couldn't."

"You weren't the only one who was in that accident, Rocco."

"I know," I mutter, feeling like an asshole.

"I lost my best friend that day. I had to deal with my grief alone."

"You had your aunt," I tell her, and I immediately regret my words.

I know all about her aunt and what a bitch she was to Rebel.

She lets out a disgusted laugh. "That woman never cared about me. She was more worried how much the hospital bill was than how I was doing or what I felt. I was alone. Totally and completely alone the moment you walked out of the emergency room."

"I…" I start to say, but I have nothing.

There's no excuse for the way I behaved. I did everything I could to try to forget the look in Carrie's eyes as her life drifted away.

No matter how hard I've tried, I've failed.

Every night when I close my eyes, I see Carrie's face, hear her gasp for air, and watch her die all over again. Every. Fucking. Night.

"I know we only knew each other for a short time, but damn it, I thought you'd at least pick up the phone when I called." She shifts in the seat, finally facing me with her back plastered against the door. "I thought if anyone knew how I felt, after the way you were with me in the hospital, it would be you. You'd be there. You'd listen. You'd help. You'd somehow make things better. A man who doesn't care doesn't sit at someone's hospital bedside, holding them, comforting them, just to turn his back. Or at least, that's what I thought…until you did."

Her words sting, slicing through me like a piece of glass tearing through cloth. "I was an asshole."

"Well, at least we can agree on something." She scoffs, turning her face toward the windshield, folding her arms across her chest.

"I relive that day every night when I go to sleep," I admit, something I've done with no one else in my life, not even my brother.

"You do?" she asks, but this time, her voice is gentler.

I keep a lot to myself. Carmello doesn't need to know the gory details. He already has the burden of Carrie's death on his shoulders; he doesn't need my baggage to weigh him down any further.

"Yeah," I whisper, staring out at the open road in front of us. "Every fucking night, I see her face and watch her die all over again."

I almost flinch when Rebel's soft fingers touch my forearm, catching me by surprise at how gently she's touched me. "I'm sorry," she whispers back. "That's awful. I should've been awake. I should've been the one comforting her."

"No," I snap. "It's something you wouldn't have

been able to shake. I thought you were dead too at first, that day," I confess, moving my gaze from the road to her for a moment. "When I looked at you, you were slumped over, and I couldn't move with Carrie in my lap until..." I swallow the bile and terror that rise in my throat every time I replay those moments in my mind. "I was helpless to save her, and if I would've lost you too, I don't know..."

"You couldn't have saved her, Rocco. No one could have."

"I know."

She tightens her fingers on my arm. "I'm serious. You couldn't have saved her."

"I know, sugar."

"Do you?" she asks softly, her hand still on me.

I didn't know that then. I blamed myself, thinking I should've been able to MacGyver something to give Carrie the ability to breathe.

"I do. I know I couldn't have saved her life. But watching someone die is nothing like in the movies. Seeing it firsthand is something a person never forgets, and Rebel, I never forgot."

I wish I could pull off to the side of the road and haul Rebel into my arms, wrapping myself in her goodness and forcing the bad out of my head, replacing it with only good.

"At least she didn't die alone. You gave her comfort when she needed it the most."

"It wasn't enough," I argue.

"What happened to you?" Rebel asks, sliding her

soft palm up and down my forearm. "You were always so full of life and happy when I knew you."

"Part of me died that day too."

"There's a sadness that clings to you now. I wouldn't have believed Carrie's death was so life-altering for you, but seeing you now, I feel it."

How could I be the same?

Death hugs a person like a second skin, never leaving them after they feel it coating their soul.

"I'm still happy," I tell her. "I know how lucky I am for every day I get walking around, doing my thing. The three of us were lucky as fuck to survive. My view of life and my mortality changed that day, though."

"Mine too," she says, dropping her hand from my arm, breaking the contact I wanted and needed so badly, but didn't realize I did. A loud sigh comes from her lips before she continues. "I decided I wasn't going to live another moment being alone and sad. I spent the first twenty years of my life like that, and I wasn't going to do it anymore. I made that promise to myself and to Carrie."

I think we all did that. We all made promises to ourselves and others. Mine was to never fall in love, hitching myself to someone who could rip my heart out, dying like Carrie.

"And how did that work out for you?" I mutter, and then I wince because I've been a total dick and I am continuing down that road with an asshole comment like that.

"You're just a giant grumpy jerk now, aren't you?

You're miserable and want to pass that shit on to everyone else. Is that your thing? Just being a dick?"

"Rebel," I say in a pleading voice, "I'm really not. I didn't mean to say that. It was wrong of me. I'm sorry."

"You say you're sorry a lot, but do you ever really mean what you say anymore?" she asks.

That stings, but she isn't wrong.

I glance to the side, staring at her for a second. "I do mean it."

"Then act like it. No more shitty comments or snark."

"Snark?" I ask.

No one's ever called me snarky. A dick or an asshole, yes, but never snarky. Nope.

"There're a dozen adjectives I could use to describe you, and snarky does fit, along with assho—"

I grunt. "I get it. There's still part of me that's the same cocky hunk you met ten years ago."

"Cocky hunk," she mumbles and laughs. "I see your opinion of yourself hasn't changed."

I ignore her comment and keep on rolling. She can call me whatever she wants as long as it gets her talking about the things we need to know. "I want to help you. I *need* to help you."

She rolls her eyes. "You didn't have to take us with you. You could've left Adaline and me at the cabin. We would've figured things out. I've been on my own for most of my life, and somehow, I've managed to survive. We would've been fine. I've never needed anyone."

"Absolutely not," I tell her.

She's a girl. A capable one, but she isn't going to be able to fend off some creepy asshole who is looking for her, with a kid attached to her hip.

She needs men, or at least a man—me, specifically —to make sure she stays safe and keeps breathing.

"I would've found somewhere else safe for us to go."

"You found some place. You're with me now. You have *us*."

She looks at me funny, her lip curling up. "I don't have the two of you, and I'm not with you, with you. I'm a charity case at this point. Something I don't deal well with and never have."

I lift an eyebrow, glancing at her. "Do I look that fucking generous to take on a charity case?"

She studies me, her blue eyes raking across my face. "No. You still look like an asshole."

I smirk, giving her a wink. "The fire's still there, sugar. You can't deny it. You feel it, don't you? Still feel me inside you after all these years."

"The fire is barely an ember now, Rocco. And as for your dick…" She pauses, and I know she's going to say something shitty, but when she squeezes her legs together, I know I've got her.

She still feels me buried deep.

There's a satisfaction in it that I can't describe, but it's fucking magnificent.

"Whatever you need to tell yourself. But while we're talking, want to tell me why you're running?"

She sighs, pinching the bridge of her nose as she

rests her right side against the door. "After Carrie died, I went wild. I don't even know how I'm still alive except for the simple fact that I got pregnant and decided to clean up my act."

Her admission isn't shocking. I spent more than enough time doing dumb-ass shit, not caring if I lived or died until my father righted my ass. He helped me channel my rage and helplessness into something more productive and safer.

"And then what happened?" I ask her, hoping she'll keep talking.

She turns her face away so I can't see her eyes. "I got married."

Those words are like a punch to the gut, but they shouldn't be. Ten years is a long time, and I didn't expect her to wait for me since I sure as hell wasn't waiting for her. "Wait. Carmello said you had an ex-boyfriend you're running from. Not a husband?"

She pulls at a string at the bottom of her shirt. "I married Collin almost six years ago. He's Adaline's biological father, but he died before her first birthday."

"I'm sorry," I say and mean those words.

"We didn't love each other." She glances my way, sadness all over her face. "After he died, I was alone with Adaline for a long time, scraping to get by, and then I met Beau. He was nice at first, but then he changed. First, it was only his words that hurt, but then…"

I brace myself.

I know the next words out of her mouth are going to set me off.

They should set any man off. No man should ever lay his hands on a woman.

Never.

My fingers tighten around the steering wheel, and I sit up a little straighter but somehow keep my mouth shut.

It isn't the time to insert my foot or chide her for getting involved with an abusive prick. Men are good at hiding their shitty personalities until the girl is in too deep to leave.

"He only hit me once, and I packed my things and we left. I'd had enough bad in my life. I wasn't about to stick around for more."

My chest aches and fire burns inside my veins, but I keep my voice even, controlling myself. "You deserve so much better than that, Reb."

"I called you after Collin died, you know," she says softly. "I was in trouble, and I couldn't think of anyone else to call except you. But when you didn't answer…"

"Fuck," I hiss. "Now I feel like an even bigger asshole than I already did. If I'd known…"

What would I have done? Offered her another I'm sorry? Leaving her in the dust, most likely.

"You didn't know, couldn't know, and I didn't leave a message to tell you."

"I should've at least picked up the phone. I saw your name flash on the screen, and I froze. I was a dumbass."

"I won't argue with that." She gives me a small smile when I look her way.

"Then what happened?" I ask, needing to know more and not wanting to linger on all the ways I've fucked up.

"There's nothing more to say. I had Adaline and lived off his life insurance for a while. Then I met Beau, and shit went south in a hurry. I called Carmello, looking for a place to get back on my feet and hide out for a little while. And now here I am, sitting in your truck."

I know there's a hell of a lot she's leaving out, but I don't press her. She'll tell me when she's ready, and I know she isn't going anywhere for a hot minute.

"Do you think he'll come after you?"

She shrugs. "I don't know. It's not like he was in love with me or her, but anything is possible. He was starting to get more possessive, and not in that fun and sexy way either."

"I won't let anything happen to you," I promise her. "You two are staying with me for as long as you want. No argument, Rebel. Until we know if he'll come for you or we eliminate him as a threat, you're at my house."

"I don't think—"

I shake my head. "There's nothing to think about."

"But—" She lifts a finger.

I give her a look, and she drops her hand back to her lap. "You want to live?"

"Yes." She frowns, narrowing her eyes.

"You want to never have to look over your shoulder again, wondering if he's there for you two?"

"Of course." She sighs, sinking down into the seat.

"Then you're at my house, sugar. No ifs, ands, or buts about it. Under my roof is the safest place for you to be."

"We'll cramp your style."

"I don't have a style."

"You'll see. You'll kick us out in a week."

"I'd never do that. You're stuck with me now. Until I know you're safe, I'm not letting you out of my sight."

"Fucking fabulous," she mutters into the window, bringing a smile to my face.

I don't want to admit it, but although I am kicking myself for not answering the phone in the past, this is the first time in ten years I've felt any semblance of normalcy. And it has everything to do with her.

8

REBEL

"WE CAN JUST STAY THERE." I POINT TO THE SMALL hotel on the corner as we sit at the traffic light. "It'll be easier for everyone."

Especially me and my heart.

The feelings I had for Rocco haven't faded, no matter how many times I've told myself they did.

Sitting this close to him and alone, I haven't stopped buzzing with excitement.

He still has a pull, one I can't shake, and my body has never forgotten the way he touched me.

"Nope," he snaps with the slightest shake of his head. "Not happening. I need to keep an eye on you."

Keep an eye on me?

I blink, hoping I heard him wrong.

Rocco always was bossy, but this is extreme, and I am not digging it.

Not at all.

"Excuse me?" I ask, turning my head to the side and glaring at him. "Keep an eye on me?"

"Rebel…"

"No. No. No. I don't need a keeper, Rocco." I roll my eyes and wave my hand in his direction. "Didn't have one for my childhood, and I sure as fuck don't need one now."

"Be fucking serious and think about this shit. You could be in some real trouble. I'd be worried if you were in a hotel and alone. Don't you want Adaline to have someplace comfortable and safe to stay?"

He has a point.

One I don't like to admit.

He's right.

If I were alone, I could hide away easier and figure out how to keep myself safe.

But Adaline adds a new level of complication.

I can't check us in to a seedy hotel where hookers and johns pay by the hour to "rent" a room.

It won't do, but neither will staying at Rocco's, having him "keep an eye" on me.

I know myself well enough to know we'll fall right back to where we left off.

Our limbs tangled.

Him inside me.

My toes curling.

Tons of orgasms.

Is that so bad? No, but my heart can't take much more hurt, and Rocco has the ability to obliterate whatever little sliver I still have left.

I can resist him for Adaline. I can stop myself from rolling up on my toes, wrapping my arms around his neck, and planting my lips on his.

I can do that, right?

I have to for her. She deserves a clean room, a safe place, and anything else I am being offered.

"Yes," I blurt out, angry with myself and him for using my kid against me. He knew I couldn't disagree with him. It was a low blow and completely effective. "Of course I do."

"I have a nice house with a spare bedroom, a pool, and a fenced-in yard for the kid to play in." He tips his head toward the hotel, and it is indeed shitty, but he could've had his privacy without the extra baggage of a chick he slept with years ago and her kid. "Sounds a hell of a lot better than that shady-ass hotel, yeah?"

"Yeah," I mutter. "I guess, but it's pretty damn close."

"We're only a few miles away from my house, and then you can settle in for however long you want or need to stay."

"But what about your girlfriend?" I ask, immediately regretting the question because it sounds like I am fishing for information.

Am I fishing? A small part of me wants to know... needs to know.

He's still as handsome as he used to be. Time has been really freaking good to him, just like his brother. His body has filled out, becoming more of a man since the last time I laid both eyes and hands on him.

He is hot, and that pisses me off.

"No girlfriend."

My gaze moves up his arm, paying close attention to the ridges of the muscles as they bulge under his skin and trying to tamp down the lust curling inside me. "No?"

"No," he grunts.

"Why?"

Ugh.

I *am* fishing for information.

I couldn't be any more transparent, but he doesn't flinch at the question. Thank God.

"Relationships lead to feelings, and feelings lead to heartbreak."

I gape at him, knowing he isn't the same guy I was with before. "That's a pessimistic way to look at love, Rocco."

I've had bad luck in the relationship department, but I'm not closing off my heart to possibilities in the future.

There is someone out there for me. There has to be happiness at the end of all this, or what's the point.

Life has to be more than pain.

He adjusts himself in the driver's seat, his lips pulling down at the edges. "Never been in love, and never plan to be either. Easier that way. Safer."

"I don't have the best track record, but I can't stop believing there's someone out there for me. Though, maybe you're right. Maybe I am meant to be alone and miserable. I have Adaline, and she gives me enough joy to fill my life."

"You've just had shit luck with men, Rebel."

That is putting my love life mildly. I can't remember one who was worth a damn. Even Collin, God rest his soul, was marginal at best. Beau sucked. And then all the guys I'd been with before, no one had any redeeming qualities other than a stiff dick. Except for one, and he is sitting next to me.

Don't go there, Rebel.

He already made it pretty damn clear he isn't going to fall in love with anyone, and that includes me. He isn't about to change his ways because I've fallen into his lap when he wasn't looking for me and didn't really want me around.

He is honorable. A decent human being and that's why my ass is planted next to him. Not out of some allegiance, loyalty, or love.

"And in the same respect, you have no way of knowing if you'll have your heart broken. I hate that Beau was my life, even if for only the briefest time. Then there's Collin, but..." My voice drifts as I stare into the side mirror at Carmello's red car. "I wouldn't have Adaline if it weren't for him. So sometimes, the most beautiful things come from the worst mistakes."

There's nothing but silence after my last statement, only the rumble of the engine as we head down a tree-lined street to a cute white house flanked by the most beautiful birds-of-paradise and hibiscus bushes.

I lean forward, getting a better look as he pulls into the driveway and stops the SUV. "This is your place?"

"Yep."

"It's so…" I smile, glancing over at the grumpy big guy, wondering how he has such a pretty yard. "…colorful."

"My mother designed the landscaping."

That makes total sense. He doesn't look like the type to work for hours pruning bushes and planting new flowers in every shade of the rainbow.

"Mama's boy," I whisper with a smile on my lips.

But I knew this about him too. It was clear at the hospital when she came running in, ready to swoop in to protect and care for her fully grown son.

He shrugs. "You can't tell her no. I tried. Trust me. The woman doesn't know what it means."

"Well, she did a beautiful job."

His place is much nicer than the shitty hotel down the street. And if the rest of the house looks anything like the outside, staying with Rocco isn't going to be the worst thing in the world for my little girl and our safety, but I wonder how it will be for my heart.

Carmello pulls in behind us as I hop out and my feet hit the pristine gray cement. His eyes are wide, and I can see Adaline talking her head off behind him.

He's probably near his breaking point because I've had that look on my face plenty of times, especially after hours in the car with her.

Carmello's door swings open, and one long, thick, denim-covered leg pokes out before the rest of his tall body follows. "Jesus," he mutters, shutting the door and leaving Adaline inside. "The kid can talk."

I giggle as I walk toward him, ready to fish my girl out of his car. "Told you."

He grabs his head, shaking it. "You did, but you didn't explain the length and depth of her ability to speak for hours and hours without so much as taking a breath."

I stop in front of him, tipping my head back, trying not to laugh in his face. "No. No. I *told* you she would talk the entire way."

"She should come with a warning label," he says, but there's a small smirk on his face.

He can say what he wants, but I know Carmello well enough to know he was probably just like Adaline as a child. He's a chatterbox, unlike his more aloof and grumpy-as-hell twin brother.

"Mommy!" Adaline yells from inside the car. "Mommy!"

"I better get her," I tell him before moving around his wide body to the door.

"I'll grab your things and put them in Rocco's house," he says behind me.

"Thank you, but I can grab them."

"Stop," Carmello replies. "Just grab the kid. I got the bags."

I open the door to find Adaline with her arms extended and singing some song no child has any business singing.

"Wiggle, wiggle," Adaline chirps, almost leaping

into my arms as I unbuckle her from the car seat. "You booty…"

My hand lands on her mouth before she has a chance to continue the song. I narrow my gaze at Carmello. "What the heck were you listening to?" I ask him as soon as Adaline's in my arms and we're clear of his car.

He lifts one shoulder and looks away from me, knowing full well he's busted, but he'll dig in. It's one thing I learned about the Caldo men in the short amount of time I spent with them years ago. They have a hard time admitting when they've fucked up. And this time, he's fucked up. "Snoop and Jason Derulo. Best song ever."

Adaline wiggles her bottom in my arms, shimmying down my body, and takes off as I keep my eyes pinned on Carmello. "Seriously? She's five."

"Start 'em young and right, Reb. You know this. She doesn't even know what she's singing anyway."

"But everyone else will," I explain to a man who's never had a child.

He waves his hand, brushing me off. "She'll forget it before she falls asleep tonight."

My steely stare hardens. "Are you new? She'll remember those words for days and days. Fuck."

He laughs and moves past me again, carrying the bags toward the house. "Look at them." He ticks his head toward the corner of the house, and my eyes follow.

Rocco's kneeling, and Adaline's at his side, touching

his shoulder. She's leaning forward, smelling an orange flower, while Rocco speaks so softly to her, I can't hear their conversation.

My heart seizes at how cute they are together.

I know my daughter misses having a father in her life. I missed out on that experience too, and now, so is my kid.

All because I picked shitty men.

"Cute, huh?" Carmello smiles.

"Precious," I say in a sarcastic tone, but my insides are a jumbled mess.

Watching them interact makes my chest ache. The burn is so deep, I'm not sure I'll ever get the feeling to go away. She deserves to have a man look at her every day the way Rocco is watching her, smiling at her cute little face.

"Lighten up," Carmello tells me, nudging me with his elbow. "Things can only get better."

"Sure," I mutter, following him toward the front door of the house.

"Yo. I got shit to do, bro!" Carmello yells out to Rocco, who quickly rises to his feet, taking Adaline by the hand and leading her in our direction.

I expect her to let go of him, but she adjusts her grip, only holding his hand tighter.

They look so natural together.

If I didn't know better, I'd think she was his.

They have the same fierce look.

Same dark hair and tanned complexion.

In a perfect world, she would have been his and not

Collin's, but nothing about my life has ever gone the easy way.

"Wiggle. Wiggle." Adaline's still singing, holding on to Rocco's hand like he's her tether to the ground.

"See," I say, motioning toward her and still glaring at the smiling Carmello. "You did that."

Carm winks at Adaline, not helping the situation. "I'm not sorry. The kid knows good music when she hears it."

"Ugh," I mumble, rolling my eyes.

"Mommy," Adaline whispers and grabs on to my hand, holding both Rocco's and mine at the same time. "Is this where we live now?"

Her eyes are big, filled with so much hope and excitement, it hurts me to be the one who has to kill all that joy.

"We're just visiting for a few days," I tell her, gently squeezing her fingers.

She tips her head back farther and peers up at Rocco. "Only a few days?" she asks him with a giant pout on her face.

The kid is good.

She knows how to work the guilt and her pretty face.

I am in for a world of hurt when she gets older. Well, I am already in that world, and she hasn't even started attending school.

She can charm the last coins out of an old lady's pocketbook with her smile and a please.

Rocco places the key in the lock and casually tips his head down. I can see the second he sees her pout and gets sucked in by the cuteness. "You can stay as long as you want, princess."

My eyes flash with annoyance, but he's not looking at me.

He's given her hope when there isn't any, and I'll be the one left to pick up the pieces...again.

Her frown disappears, replaced by a huge smile. "And Mello?" She glances to my side where Rocco's brother is standing, holding the suitcases, jostling back and forth on his feet like he has ants in his pants.

"I'll visit, squirt," he tells her, giving her the sweetest, soft smile. "Good?"

She nods. "Yep."

Fucking fabulous.

Two good guys, not realizing they are going to break her heart. Rocco already broke mine, and now they both are going to do it to her.

Rocco opens the door and goes to take a step inside, opening his fingers like he's going to release Adaline's hand, but she's having none of it. She moves with him, keeping a death grip on his hand but releasing mine.

I feel a small pang of jealousy, but I try to push it away. She must be starving for the affection only a father can give. She has me all the time, but even I get bored with myself, as I'm sure she does too, which is obvious by the way she's clinging to both Caldo men.

"I'm going to throw these in the spare room and head out," Carmello tells me.

I only nod in response, too busy looking around.

The inside of Rocco's home is not girlie like the outside.

It's rich, with deep tones of brown and black, leather furniture, and lots of wood everywhere.

There's not a feminine touch in sight, and since he doesn't and has never had a girlfriend, he has his place the way he wants it.

I like the more modern, contemporary edge. I never did frilly. I'm not into flowers, lace, throw pillows, and all the useless shit so many of my friends are. I don't care if I have the softest throw rug; I'm just happy if I have a couch that doesn't have a hole in the cushion.

"Nice place," I tell Rocco as he walks to the other end of the living room, Adaline still attached to him, and places his keys on the coffee table.

"Thanks," he says, peering down at Adaline and where their bodies are attached.

Adaline yanks on his hand, and he leans over as she beckons his face closer. "I have to go potty."

"Down the hall, sweetie," he tells her, ticking his head across the room. "Can you go alone?"

She immediately nods and skips away, leaving us staring at each other in awkward silence.

Carmello breezes out of the hallway, phone in his hand, typing away like mad. "I'm late for my date. You kids have fun tonight."

"You sure you don't want to stay?" I ask, almost pleading with him not to leave me alone...leave us alone.

"You two will be fine. You've had *fun* before." He

smirks, his eyes moving from me to his brother. "Behave."

Rocco shakes his head. "Food and bed. That's all I care about. I'm exhausted."

My belly immediately growls at the mention of food, and Rocco's eyes slide to me, missing nothing.

"Pizza!" Adaline exclaims as she comes back down the hall, always wanting pizza. She'd eat it every day without complaint if I allowed her.

"Pizza it is." Rocco doesn't realize it, but he just cemented his awesomeness even more in Adaline's eyes.

"Later," Carmello calls out before slamming the door behind him, leaving us alone.

"Bath and bed right afterward, Adaline," I tell her.

"Okay, Mom," she groans, sounding sad and defeated but looking up at Rocco like he's going to rescue her.

But he shakes his head, killing her dreams. "Bedtime for all of us. We all need our rest."

"Fine." She kicks her little pink tennis shoes against his dark hardwood before lifting her big doe eyes to him. "Pizza?"

"You got it," he says with a smile, sucked right in.

Two hours later, our bellies are full, and I'm cuddled in bed with Adaline. This is the first night I'm not afraid or filled with worry as I close my eyes.

We're safe.

Beau is hopefully hundreds of miles away, not giving two shits that we aren't there anymore.

I rub Adaline's cheek with the backs of my fingers until we both drift to sleep.

I ROLL OVER, and sunshine hits my face, the warmth against my skin unmistakable. I turn, expecting to see my little girl next to me, but instead, I find nothing but an empty space and a dented pillow.

I rocket upward, a knot starting in my stomach before the panic follows up my throat.

Jumping up, I start tearing the blankets off the bed before looking over the edge, praying she's on the floor fast asleep.

But she's not.

The room is empty.

Oh God.

Oh God.

Oh God.

My heart races, and a cold sweat breaks out across the back of my neck.

There's nothing more terrifying than not knowing where your child is, and I am there.

"Adaline," I whisper, not sure what time it is or if Rocco is still asleep, but freaking the fuck out.

Walking quickly, I open every door, glance around, call out her name, and when I come up empty, I move on to the next.

"Adaline, baby. Where are you?" I say a little louder this time as I make my way down the hallway to the living room, hoping she's passed out on the couch.

Each step causes my heart to race a little faster and my stomach to twist a little tighter.

But the living room is empty too.

She's nowhere. Gone. Poof.

Fuck!

What if Beau found us and took her?

The reality of that being a possibility makes my knees weak, almost giving out underneath me, but I catch myself on the edge of the couch, trying to breathe.

He didn't find us.

We're safe.

I remind myself, repeating those words as I continue my search, calling out for Adaline over and over again, waiting for her reply.

But the house is dead silent.

As I turn, I notice the sliding glass door to the pool area is open, and my heart comes to a screeching halt, and my chest fills with nothing but emptiness.

Adaline doesn't know how to swim.

Oh my God!

I didn't even think about the fact that there's a pool only a few feet away and I have to have a talk with her about going out there without me. I run forward, pushing the sliding glass door open farther and rush toward the pool.

It's empty.

I glance around, my hands and body shaking in fear and only getting worse with every step I take.

What if she's not here?

What if he *did* find us and he took her in the middle of the night without me even waking up?

I run inside, making a mad dash for Rocco's room and don't even knock.

I open the door and immediately come to a dead stop and cover my mouth.

Oh shit.

Rocco's lying there, his eyes open, mouthing, "Help me," with Adaline curled against his bare chest, sound asleep.

9

ROCCO

Rebel's eyes widen as soon as they find Adaline.

"Help," I whisper to her, needing a rescue.

I've been lying here for damn near an hour, not moving, too scared to wake the kid.

I don't know how she got here or why she is in my bed, but when I opened my eyes, I was in utter shock.

The last thing I wanted to do was scare the child. I didn't know if she'd wake up in a panic or cry out for her mother. And I knew I didn't want to piss off Rebel either.

So, I lay here and waited.

The minutes ticked by as I studied the little girl's face.

The dip of her nose, the plumpness of her cheeks, just like her mother's.

Everything about her is a carbon copy of Rebel's beauty.

99

I don't know what her father looked like, but I know she didn't get a damn thing from him…thank God.

Rebel walks into the room, her eyes moving from me back to Adaline, the color returning to her face. "How did this happen?"

"I don't know," I whisper, remaining completely still. "She was just here when I woke up."

"She was just here?" she asks, repeating my words.

"Like I said…she was just here."

I peer down, soaking in the little girl fisting her pink blanket in her hand and curled against my chest.

"I don't understand." Rebel leans over and stares down at Adaline too.

"Me either, sugar. I went to bed alone and never thought I'd wake up the opposite."

"I didn't even feel her get out of bed. I almost had a heart attack when I woke up."

"Makes two of us." I smile but remain frozen, almost too scared to breathe, even though the kid hasn't moved, even with our whispering. "While I love the chitchat, I could use a little help, Reb. Got nothing on under this sheet, sugar."

Rebel's mouth falls open, and her eyes dip to my lower half. "What?"

"Naked as the day I was born, babe. You remember what I look like underneath this, yeah?"

Rebel's mouth opens and closes, but her eyes narrow, flashing with…lust? She definitely remembers. How could she forget? I fucked her every way possible and as many times as I could before…

"She sleeps heavy. Don't worry. You can move." Rebel slides her arms under Adaline's small body and pulls her away gently.

"Mommy," Adaline whispers, her voice deeper than usual.

Sleeps heavy, my ass.

"Hey, baby. Let's get you back to bed," Rebel says sweetly, kissing the little girl's puffy pink cheeks.

There's a part of me that goes all soft on the inside seeing this side of Rebel.

I'd never thought of her as a mom, but then again, who thinks of someone that way when you're so young?

I never would've expected her to walk back into my life, ten years after the accident, with a little girl in tow.

Adaline rubs her eyes with one hand, wiping away the sleep. "This is bed."

"This is Rocco's bed, honey. Not ours."

"It's so soft," she tells her mom, trying to inch out of her arms to slide back onto the pillow top.

Can't argue with the kid.

I spent a fuckton on the best mattress I could find. I don't do shitty, hard beds just as much as I don't do relationships. The spare room has a crappy mattress because if anyone stays over, I don't want them to be too comfortable and want to overstay their very short welcome.

Rebel drags her backward, and Adaline collapses, making herself harder to move. "Come on, sleepyhead."

"No, Mommy. I stay with Rocky."

"Rocky?" Rebel's eyes slice to me. "Who calls him Rocky?"

"Mello," Adaline whispers, finally letting Rebel lift her.

"Well, Rocky has to get up. You can't stay in his bed while he does that."

Adaline turns her face toward me as she sits in her mother's lap on the edge of my bed. Her eyelids are heavy, but those big, deep eyes stare at me like she's looking into my soul. "He's sad," the squirt whispers.

"I'm great, baby," I reassure her.

"I heard you." Her face goes all soft and cute like her voice.

My body tightens.

She heard me?

No one's heard me besides my mother the first few days after the accident.

I know I still have the nightmares, waking myself up many times over the years, cold sweat covering me and a scream tearing out of my throat.

"You heard me?" I ask, my gaze moving from Adaline to Rebel, who looks as confused as I feel.

"Yelling." She nods.

"I was?"

Fuck me.

She nods, blinking slowly. "Who's Carrie?"

That single simple question is like a punch to the gut, bringing back the nightmare I had last night and have had every night since the accident.

"Carrie was my friend, baby," Rebel tells her, sweeping Adaline's hair away from her face where it is clinging to her damp cheeks. "Rocco knew her too."

"Was she hurting you?" Adaline asks me, studying my face with such innocence in her expression. "In your dream."

I sit up, careful not to let the blankets fall below my waist. This is the first time I've ever had a conversation with a little girl and her mother while buck-ass naked. A woman I've been balls deep in before. A woman I felt something for years ago—and yet the fire that burned that night still glows deep inside me.

"She wasn't hurting me, Adaline. I promise."

"'Kay."

Rebel hugs her daughter tighter, resting her cheek against the top of Adaline's head. "It was just a bad dream. You have bad dreams too, but they're not real. Remember, baby?"

Adaline pulls away and gazes up at Rebel. "And you snuggle me to make me feel better."

"I do." Rebel brushes her lips against Adaline's forehead. "That's what you do when you love someone, baby. You chase away their sadness."

"He was sad and needed love, so I gave it to him."

The second gut-punch of the morning has officially been delivered by the kid and my feet haven't even touched the floor.

Brutal, honest truth.

Rebel's eyes meet mine, and the same sadness is in

them that was also in Adaline's. "That was sweet of you, baby," Rebel tells her, looking away from me for a moment to focus on her kid.

"Thank you," I whisper, letting Adaline know I am grateful for her sweetness. "But you didn't have to do that, squirt."

"You stopped," she replies.

I jerk my head back. "I stopped?"

"I climbed up, snuggled you, and you stopped," she explains, waving her tiny hand toward me.

"I'm sorry," I whisper, swallowing down my remorse.

"What do you say again, Mommy?" Adaline asks Rebel, tangling her fingertips around her mother's dark black hair.

"I don't know, sweetie. I say a lot of things."

Adaline smiles, lighting up the room. "Hugs make everything better."

"I do say that, don't I?" Rebel smiles down at the tiny carbon copy of herself.

Adaline's eyes brighten as the sleep seems to vanish from her tiny frame. "I'm thirsty."

"Come on, monkey. Let's get you something to drink." Rebel climbs to her feet and takes Adaline with her, giving me a quick but small smile.

I just sit there, winded by the conversation, unable to form any words after everything that just transpired.

Adaline's eyes never leave mine as Rebel moves toward the bedroom door. She has her chin resting on

Rebel's shoulder, smiling at me with the sweetest little grin.

I wave, trying to keep a smile on my face too, but feeling so many emotions swirling inside me.

"Fuck," I mutter as soon as the door closes and they're both gone.

Swinging my legs off the side of the bed, I lean over, resting my elbows on my knees and staring at the floor. What the hell just happened?

The kid got under my skin.

Not in a bad way, but taking me down a road that could very well be dangerous for my heart.

I'm just about to stand when my phone starts to vibrate on the nightstand next to me. I glance over, seeing my mother's name on the screen. I wait, staring as the phone dances around my nightstand, but I'm not about to answer. She never calls this early and never for no reason.

There is one thing I know without having to pick up the phone—Carmello opened his big fat mouth, and Mom is calling to get the details.

I breathe a sigh of relief when the phone grows silent. I've bought myself a few hours before I have to face the woman who gave birth to me. She won't stop either until I tell her everything.

I don't even have one leg in my sweatpants when my phone starts again.

"Fuckin' Mello," I mutter, grabbing my phone off the nightstand. "Hey, Ma."

"Busy?" she asks without even a hello.

"Nope. Just got up."

"Alone?"

Yep.

Carmello talked.

He probably sang like a canary last night, giving up every little detail, including the fact that I insisted Rebel and Adaline stay at my house and not his.

"Yeah, Ma. Alone."

"Shame," she says, blowing out an exasperated breath. "I'm coming over."

"Ma."

"No arguing. I'm just going to drop by for a few minutes. It's been years since I've seen Rebel, and Mello told me about her little girl. I figured I could drop off a few things for her to have. He said they came with very little."

Mello and I are going to have words.

He knew exactly how Ma would be, and he was calculated with the amount of information he dropped in her lap. If she was busy with me, she wasn't watching him, telling him how to live his life.

"Fine." I sigh, resting my forehead in my hand, elbow on my knee.

"Fine?" she asks, surprise in her voice.

"Yeah, Ma. No use arguing, and whatever you can bring for Adaline would be great. She's a sweet kid."

"I heard she's a cutie and a talker too."

"She's all that and more."

"She's going to suck you in, baby."

"No one's going to suck me in, Ma, especially not a five-year-old."

"Uh-huh. Keep telling yourself whatever you want. How's Rebel?"

"Good," I say, not bothering to argue with her about Adaline, because she's right, but I'll die on that hill and never tell her how accurate her statement is.

"Still pretty?"

"More," I mutter.

"Mm-hmm," she mumbles. "You're a goner. Just don't know it yet."

"I am not."

"Never saw you with a woman the way you were with her."

"She was hurt back then, Ma. What was I supposed to do?"

"You were protective, just like we taught you to be over those you cared about, Rocco. Never seen you that way since. And based on what Carmello said, that feeling hasn't left you."

"It's gone, Ma. I'm just being nice. She needed somewhere to lay low, and I'm giving her that."

"Keep lying to yourself. See you in thirty, baby," she tells me before the line goes dead.

I curse as I pull on my sweatpants and ready myself for the insanity that's about to happen when my mother lays eyes on Rebel and Adaline.

If that kid is already pulling on my heartstrings and getting under my skin, she is going to have my mom wrapped around her pinkie in under five minutes.

Izzy Caldo is a sucker for any baby.

She is a badass too. There is no doubting that. No one messes with her, not even her brothers. But kids… they get to her every time.

I am about to be screwed and not in any way I ever thought I wanted.

10

REBEL

I BARELY HAVE MY FAVORITE PAIR OF RIPPED JEANS around my hips when the doorbell rings. I freeze, staring at the bedroom door like the boogeyman is about to walk through it, even though Rocco told me who was coming.

"Mommy." Adaline's on the floor, playing with the one doll I managed to stuff into her suitcase. "Why are you so scared?"

"I'm not scared. I'm nervous. There's a difference, baby."

"You look scared," she tells me, always watching me like a hawk and calling me out on whatever I'm doing.

Kids are great for that.

They don't hold back, and unless they've been caught doing something they shouldn't be doing, they don't lie.

At least, Adaline doesn't.

The girl tells the truth even when it is the most painful thing to hear. She doesn't have a filter and doesn't understand how sometimes her words are painful even when completely honest.

I shimmy the jeans up to my waist, fastening the zipper and button while holding in the gut I've been the proud recipient of since my pregnancy.

"Is Beau here?" she asks me, her eyes filled with fear.

I shake my head. "No. He's far away."

"Good," she whispers, continuing to play.

"Rocco's mom is here," I reply, reaching for the only sweater in my suitcase since it is a rare cold winter day in Florida.

Adaline's eyes grow wide as saucers as she drops the doll to the floor. "Rocco's mom?"

"Yep. His mom." I pull my hair up, holding it in one hand while slipping a rubber band around it. "Do I look okay?"

Adaline studies me, her curious and careful eyes soaking in every inch of me. "Very pretty."

I lean over and place a kiss on her forehead. "You're good for my ego."

"You're always pretty, Mommy."

"You're the pretty one, bug." I tap her nose. "The most beautiful girl in the world."

She giggles and blossoms with every word, growing more confident.

She climbs to her feet, the dress I put on her now with a few more wrinkles since she moved to the floor to play while I raced around the bedroom to get ready.

"Do I look okay?" she repeats back to me.

"You're beautiful too."

"I want to look beautiful for his mommy like you."

"You do, baby. You do."

Their voices carry down the hallway, low murmurs impossible to make out, yet unmistakable.

While I stand in the middle of the room, my heart racing, my feet not moving, Adaline takes it upon herself to skip around me and is out of the bedroom before I have a chance to stop her.

"Come on, Mommy," she says from the hallway and is gone in a flash, running toward the living room.

"Oh God," I whisper to no one but myself, closing my eyes and taking a deep breath.

I haven't seen Rocco's mother since the hospital. It was the one and only time I met her. She was in a complete panic, yelling at the hospital staff until she laid eyes on her son.

Two more long breaths and I open my eyes, smooth down my sweater, and walk out of the bedroom to face his mother again.

No one looks my way when I enter the living room. Adaline is standing at Rocco's side, her tiny hand in his as his mother crouches in front of her, talking softly.

The sight alone makes my eyes burn. My daughter craves attention and love, and no matter how much I give her, it isn't enough.

It isn't her fault.

Children want acceptance, and she never received it from her father.

"Well, aren't you cute as a button," Mrs. Caldo tells Adaline, tugging on the ends of her frilly pink dress. "You look like a princess."

"You're pretty too," Adaline replies, reaching out and touching her tiny fingertips to his mother's blush-covered cheeks.

His mother smiles at Adaline with so much warmth, there's a dull ache inside my chest. "Thank you. You may be the most beautiful little girl I've ever laid eyes on."

I take one step and his mother's eyes move from my daughter to me, but her smile doesn't fade. She rises to her feet, standing before her son but with a clear line of sight to where I'm standing. "Rebel," she greets me with nothing but warmth. "Honey, you look amazing."

The words are nice to hear, and even at my age, I soak them in. "Thank you, Mrs. Caldo. You're..." My eyes rake over her perfect frame, covered in an outfit I could no doubt ever afford, even after years of working at any dive bar and saving every penny. "You're stunning. I wish we'd had more..."

She walks toward me, her heels clicking against the hardwood, shaking her head. "I'll never forget that day. Come here."

I move into her embrace when her arms open, without even thinking if the behavior is normal because it feels right. "I'm sorry about all this," I tell her.

She pulls back far enough that I can see her face. "For what?"

"For being a burden on your son."

Her face softens. "You could never be a burden."

I resist the urge to laugh because I've been a burden my entire life.

After my parents died, my aunt made sure to remind me of that fact every single day I lived under her roof. My only escape was college after landing a full ride and joining a sorority, but that all fell apart after the accident.

"I think Rocco needs you as badly as you need him," she whispers to me, giving my arms a light squeeze before releasing me.

I blink at her, confused. "I doubt that."

"Mommy, look." Adaline holds up a light-brown teddy bear with dark-brown eyes and sporting a black bow tie around his neck. "Isn't it pretty?" she asks me, her other hand still firmly planted in Rocco's.

"Gorgeous, baby." I swing my gaze back to Mrs. Caldo and smile, stunned by her kind gesture. "Thank you."

Mrs. Caldo shakes her head, her long brown hair swaying with the movement. "It was no big deal. Carmello told me you were here with your little girl, and I had to come over and bring you some essentials."

"We have some stuff with us." I sound defensive when I don't mean to be. I'm grateful for the toy, but I also never want to be a charity case.

"A little girl can never have too many cute things,"

Mrs. Caldo says to me before crouching back down in front of Adaline. "What's your favorite color, princess?"

"Pink," Adaline answers.

"Next time, I'll bring you something pink, then."

"That's very kind of you, but we aren't staying," I tell her, earning a grunt followed by movement from Rocco.

"You're not leaving. It's not safe," Rocco tells me, being his bossy self, even so early in the morning.

I cover Adaline's ears with my hands and prepare for an argument. "We'll be fine. The last thing you need is an old friend and her kid sticking around, cramping your style. We're not your problem."

Mrs. Caldo's quick intake of air is unmistakable. "Oh boy," she whispers.

Rocco steps around his mother, coming to stand in front of me. "Rebel, we're not going to go over this again and again. You're safe here, and Adaline is happy here too."

"Yeah," Adaline adds, twisting her upper body while holding her new teddy bear in an embrace. "Stay here."

Rocco reaches for my hands, and I let him take them. "Once we know he's not coming for you and I'm convinced you'll be okay and you have what you need to survive, then you can leave."

I raise an eyebrow, staring into his brown eyes. "Is that an order, or are you asking me, Rocky?" I throw in that nickname, knowing full well he hates it.

Mrs. Caldo snickers behind him, leaning to the side

to give me a wink, but I remain stoic and continue my stare-down with her son.

"I'm begging you," he replies, throwing me for a loop because I never would've imagined Rocco Caldo would beg anyone to do anything.

"Just stay, dear," Mrs. Caldo says before I can reply. "Where else would you go?"

I shrug. "I don't know, but—"

"She's not going anywhere, Ma," Rocco says, squeezing my fingers which are still in his palm, "and neither is my girl." He winks at Adaline.

I glance down at the floor, unable to meet his gaze any longer, guilt filling me. "I've always been a burden. It's not a good feeling."

"Listen," Mrs. Caldo says, interrupting whatever awkward moment we're having. "Why don't you three come to dinner at the house tonight? There's nothing better than a home-cooked meal, and we can discuss this as a family."

"Ma, this isn't a family issue."

"I'm making lasagna," she says, drawing out the word in a melodic fashion, knowing her son better than anyone, along with his ability to eat.

"Ooh," Adaline says, licking her lips. "Lasagna. I love lasagna."

Mrs. Caldo leans over, scooping Adaline into her arms. "How about garlic bread? You like that too?"

"I love it." Adaline smiles, giggling when Mrs. Caldo kisses her cheek and eating up every bit of affection and attention.

"It's settled, then. The baby wants lasagna and garlic bread. The baby's going to get lasagna and garlic bread. There's nothing more to discuss. End of story."

Rocco scrubs his hand across his face. "You okay with this?" he asks me.

I shrug. "Lasagna does sound good, and—" I lean closer so only he can hear "—I'm scared of your mother."

"That makes two of us," he says, a small smile on his face. "We'll be there, Ma."

Mrs. Caldo turns in a circle, Adaline still in her arms. "Wait until James sees this one," she says to the two of us. "He's going to go bananas."

"I love bananas too," Adaline says, super cute, fishing for food.

Mrs. Caldo kisses her cheek again. "I'll buy some. How about banana pudding?"

"Yum!" Adaline exclaims.

"Thank you," is all I can say.

I haven't had a home-cooked meal I didn't cook myself in years. The idea of going to the Caldo house and being spoiled for a little while doesn't sound like the worst thing in the world.

"You're welcome, Rebel. I'm so happy to see you're looking well. The last time I saw you, curled up with…"

"Ma," Rocco warns, his gaze dipping to Adaline. "Let's not talk about that day."

Mrs. Caldo leans forward, placing Adaline's feet back on the wood floor. "Got it." She smiles at her son, but it's not joyful. "I'll see you three around seven."

"We'll be there," I say to her with nothing but happiness. "Will Carmello be there?"

"Mello!" Adaline exclaims. "Pink car. Wiggle. Wiggle. Wiggle."

"Pink car?" Mrs. Caldo looks confused, ignoring all the wiggles.

"She insists he has a pink car, and you know how much Carmello loves that." Rocco laughs, running his hand over the top of Adaline's hair playfully.

"Pink," she argues, pouting and sticking out her chin because no one's going to convince her of anything different.

"Whatever you say, kid." He shrugs with a sigh. "It's whatever color you say it is."

"You learn faster than your brother, sweetheart," Mrs. Caldo tells him, leaning in to give her son a big kiss. "I'll see you tonight."

When she's done kissing him, she moves back to me with her arms open. "I can't wait to have two more girls in the house," she whispers in my ear.

I smile, but there's a knot in my stomach. She's so kind and loving, but she makes it sound like we're sticking around, which we're not. But I can't break her heart, at least not yet. "Thank you," is all I can say, repeating those words as often as Rocco says "I'm sorry" to me.

As Mrs. Caldo moves toward the door, Adaline rushes after her. "Hug," she pleads, wiggling her arms in the air.

"How could I forget, my little princess?" Mrs. Caldo

says, wrapping Adaline in a giant hug and kissing her cheek.

"Sucker," Rocco says like he's somehow immune to her charms, when I've seen Adaline work her magic on him in the short amount of time we've been here.

His mom gives him a hard look over Adaline's shoulder, and Rocco raises his hand in surrender.

"Pussy," I whisper, giggling.

"We'll see how ballsy you are with her, Rebel. She's not easy to say no to."

"Oh, I know. But I don't pretend to be tough and then crumble with so much as a look."

"You will," he laughs back. "Oh, sugar, you so will."

Damn it.

I have a feeling this entire family will have me sucked in before I know what hits me. I'm not sure my heart can take the loss of their absence if I allow any of them to get too close.

This is just dinner.

Our stay here is only temporary.

Do not get sucked in.

Do not fall in love.

And absolutely do not kiss Rocco Caldo.

But fuck...I want to kiss his lips more than ever before, letting him sweep me away like he did so long ago.

11

ROCCO

My father sits across from me in his big leather chair, rubbing his hand slowly up and down his jeans and giving me his notoriously hard stare. "You know what you're doing?"

"Not a damn clue," I answer honestly.

The man can spot a lie from a mile away and would see through my bullshit no matter how hard I tried to be convincing.

There is a hint of a smile on his lips before it vanishes. "I looked into the man."

"And?" I lean forward, resting my elbows on my knees and bracing myself for whatever dirt he has been able to dig up on Beau.

"He's trash."

I hold my father's gaze, not shaken by the little bit of information he's just given me. "Well, obviously. That's not telling me anything I couldn't already guess."

119

"He has a rap sheet going back ten years, and it's as long as my arm."

"Violent crimes or petty shit?" I ask.

"A mix."

"Domestic violence?"

My father's nod is small, but there. "Neighbors called the cops a few times on him. He was arrested and processed once, but when it got to the hearing, the girl never showed."

"Damn," I mutter, shaking my head. "Anything else?"

"Mostly theft. Looks like he's out to make cash but without ever holding a job. I've seen the type a million times in my line of work. All about the easy money."

I straighten, resting my back against the chair. "Think I can buy him off?"

"Probably, but a man like him doesn't seem the type to care about a deal or a handshake. They always come back for more."

"I'll make him care."

My father laughs. "Oh, to be young and naïve."

"I'm neither," I tell him, raising my hand to my chin, stroking the stubble near my jaw. "Every man has a price, and since he doesn't care about Adaline, I'm sure his isn't that high."

He stands and walks toward a shelf where he's set up a few bottles of booze and glasses. "You like this girl, yeah?" he asks with his back to me as he pours two drinks.

"I don't know, Dad. We had something a long time

ago. We barely know each other."

"Your mother and I didn't either when I knew."

I stare at him as he lifts the two glasses filled with amber liquid and stalks my way so gracefully, the contents barely move.

"As soon as I laid eyes on her, there was no other woman in the world who could hold my attention. Your mother fought it, of course, but nothing and no one was going to stop me from having her. But she wanted me as much as I craved her."

"That's not how Mom tells it," I say, taking a glass from his hand.

"Your mother lies, son."

I raise my eyebrows, trying to hold back my laughter. "Doubt you'd be saying that if she were in the room," I challenge him on his statement.

"I would, and she couldn't deny it. I got her, didn't I? And she wasn't an easy get."

"It's more complicated with Rebel."

"Sure," he mumbles into his glass before taking a sip and relaxing back into his chair. "I forgot how easy it was to chase after your mother with the MC and DEA breathing down our necks. Then there was Rooster…"

"Rooster?" I ask, never having heard the name before.

He waves his glass slowly in front of us. "He's not important," he says before continuing, totally glossing over the name. "Nothing in life worth having is easy."

"Wait." I tip my head, blinking at my father because is he telling me to… Nah. My father isn't the type to ever get in my business, especially not my love life or lack thereof. "Hold up. Are you saying you think I should be with her?"

My father stares at me, barely moving a muscle. I know he's studying my every movement. The man reads people for a living, and although I'm his son, right now, I'm the mark.

"I'm saying to follow your heart, something you haven't done in ten years."

"That's not true," I argue.

He places the glass on his leg, looking as chill as if we're talking about football. "Been watching you follow your dick around. At some point, you have to grow the fuck up, settle down, and start a family."

"I'm pretty sure you followed your dick around for a lot longer than I have."

My father laughs, his face going soft. "My life didn't lend itself to stability. I was just trying to keep your uncle alive and the mission going, but the first chance I had after your mother came along, I grabbed it and never looked back."

The doors to my father's study burst open, and Adaline comes running in, waving a piece of paper and squealing, "Rocky. Rocky!"

I grab her by the waist as she comes to a stop in front of me. "Whatcha got there, princess?"

She shoves her drawing in my face. "It's Mello's *pink* car." She giggles, her eyes sliding to the doorway, where Carmello is perched against the frame, arms crossed, pretending to be pissed.

"It's red," he groans, but there's a small, barely visible smirk on his face.

He likes the kid. Doesn't matter that she says his car is pink; he likes her for it anyway. Probably the only female on the planet who could get away with those words, because how could you resist a face as cute as hers?

I pluck the paper from her hands. "It's such a pretty car."

"A *pink* car." She jostles back and forth on her tiptoes, eyes moving from me to Carmello and back. She leans in, motioning for me to move closer to her. "Pretend," she whispers.

"It's a pretty pink car," I repeat, throwing in the pink to make her happy.

How could I not want to see the kid smile? When she looks at me with those big blue eyes, I'd say just about anything to keep the smile on her face.

"You're a goner," Dad whispers.

"Addy, leave Rocco and Mr. Caldo alone, baby. They're busy talking," Rebel says, walking into the room and leaning down to grab Adaline.

Adaline twists, moving away from Rebel's hands. "No, Mommy. I stay here," she says and throws herself at me, wrapping her arms around my neck.

"He's busy," Rebel tells her, grabbing Adaline by the waist, but Addy just doubles down and holds me tighter.

"No."

I chuckle even though I know I shouldn't. She's

disobeying, but she's so stinking cute, and the fact that she doesn't want to let me go isn't so bad either.

I peer up at Rebel and smile, taking in the dip in the middle of her upper lip, remembering how soft her mouth was on mine. "It's okay, Reb. We were done. The squirt can stay."

Rebel straightens and releases her hold on Adaline, but when her eyes meet mine, I can tell she's not overly thrilled that I'm giving in to the kid's whims. "Are you sure?"

My dad stands and clears his throat. "We're done. Let's go back into the living room with the rest of the family," he says, looking directly at my mother when he says those words.

"That would be nice," she tells him. "We do have company."

"I hate to be a bother," Rebel says, her eyes moving from me to my father. "I'm sorry if—"

He holds up his hand to stop her. "Don't be sorry. We were just catching up. We should've stayed out there with the family anyway."

"Rebel, baby, you didn't do anything wrong. Stop apologizing. Caldo women never apologize." Mom looks at Dad, smiling at him.

"That shit's the truth," I mutter.

"Would you like dessert?" Ma asks, clearly not hearing me.

"If it's not you, baby, then I'm not interested," Dad answers.

Carmello and I gag a little, but Rebel smiles.

"It's apple pie." Mom raises a dark eyebrow. "Still not interested?"

"Warm or cold?"

"Warm."

"Ice cream?" he asks as he moves her way.

"Would I serve warm apple pie without ice cream?" She waves her hand at him and spins around, stalking out of the room with him hot on her heels.

Carmello gives me a quick chin lift before leaving the study right behind our parents. Rebel and I are left alone after Adaline jumps out of my lap and skips after Carmello, chanting *pink, pink, pink.*

"Everything okay?" Rebel asks me.

I stand, towering over her, and place my hands on her arms. "We were talking about a few things."

She tips her head back, eyes on me. "Were you talking about me?"

"No, sugar. We weren't," I kind of lie. "Just some other family business."

"Are you sure?" she asks, swallowing roughly and bringing her hands to my biceps.

Without thinking, I wrap my arms around her. "Completely."

"I'm sure you always dreamed a woman with a little girl would land on your doorstep with nowhere else to go. It's what every single twentysomething man fantasizes about."

I move my hands to her cheeks, tipping her head back so she can see my face. "Rebel—" I run my thumb along her bottom lip "—you've been in my fantasies since the last time I saw you."

Her lips part, and her eyes hold mine. "Don't lie," she whispers as her breathing slows.

"Not lying, Reb. Been there every day and every night for ten years."

She slides her hand between us, placing her palm on my T-shirt right over my heart. "Not all the memories are happy ones, though."

"No. They're not all happy. But I remember riding in the ambulance with you, thinking you were going to die too. I remember the panic I felt. The helplessness that ate at my insides." I sigh, pushing down the knot trying to form in my stomach. "I can't explain how relieved I was when they said you were going to be okay."

Her hand moves higher until the warmth of her fingers grazes my jaw. "I'm sorry you went through that. I'm sorry you were alone when Carrie died, but I'll never be sorry you were there to hold my hand. When I opened my eyes, I was terrified, but when I saw your face, I knew…I just knew I was going to be okay."

"Rebel…" I lean forward, wanting and needing to taste her lips.

"You two coming out or what?" Trace, my asshole younger brother, says right before our lips touch. "Mom's asking."

The moment is lost. Rebel steps back, and her hand falls from my face, leaving my body cold.

"We're coming," I growl, wanting to punch Trace in

his pretty face.

He tilts his head and smirks, eyes trained on me and not on Rebel as she moves toward him. "What's wrong, Roc?"

"Nothing," I grunt, stalking in his direction.

He grins at me, not moving.

I jab his chest, glaring at him. "You're a shithead for doing that."

"For what?" He shrugs, feigning innocence, and glances down where my finger still lingers between his pecs.

"You know exactly what you did," I say softly, knowing my mother's now within earshot, and the woman has the craziest hearing ever.

He laughs before rolling back and sauntering into the dining room like his shit doesn't stink. Being the baby of the family has done crazy things for his ego, and with every day that passes, he seems to get cockier and cockier too.

"Adaline, do you want whipped cream or ice cream with your pie?" Ma asks Adaline as she climbs up on Rebel's lap.

"Yes, please."

"So, both?" Ma smiles, loving an eater and kids. Adaline is like the killer combo.

"Yes, ma'am," Adaline replies as I slide into the chair next to her.

"A lot or a little?" Ma asks, always the one to give us options.

"A lot," Adaline says, stretching her arms out as

wide as they can go and smiling at my mother, knowing she's going to get her way too.

The kid has half the family wrapped around her little finger in twenty-four hours. My mother was a no-brainer, but the rest of us weren't a forgone conclusion. Maybe it's because we're a house of men. My poor mother always wanted a little girl, but instead had three shitheads who were more interested in wrestling than playing dress-up.

"A girl after my own heart," Ma says while piling on the ice cream and then the whipped cream before placing the giant dish in front of Adaline and Rebel. "There ya go, baby."

"That's a lot," Rebel says, her eyes wide. "She's going to be bouncing off the walls all night."

"No, I won't, Mommy," Adaline argues, grabbing the fork and digging in before anyone can take it from her.

"So, Rebel," Ma says as she gives me a plate with a smaller slice and much less whipped cream and ice cream than she gave Adaline. "There're lots of job opportunities around here. In fact, we could use—"

"Ma," I warn, knowing she's fishing for information because it's what she always does.

My mother lifts her hands up, shrugging. "What?"

"You're being nosy," I tell her.

She laughs and swats her hand in the air. "I'm being friendly. There's a difference."

"Sure," I mumble.

Rebel's warm palm lands on my leg under the table,

giving it a little squeeze. "It's okay," she says to me before turning her attention back to my ma.

"We could use a new front desk person at the shop. I've been going in a few days a week to help out, but I'm getting too old for that now."

"I don't know, Mrs. Caldo."

"Think about it, honey. You'd be doing me a favor."

"I don't know if this is where we should settle."

"Where would you go?" Ma asks.

"I don't know. I don't have any family, so we could go anywhere."

"Oh, honey, you can't live that way with a kid. You need to stay here and—"

"Izzy," Dad warns her now, giving her the side-eye as he holds his forkful of pie in front of his lips. "The woman is an adult."

"I know. I know," Ma says, pushing her hair back away from her shoulders. "It's nice to have two more girls at the table. I'd hate to see her go if she doesn't have to."

"Oh boy," Carmello mutters. "Here we go."

"It's nice to be wanted, Mrs. Caldo." Rebel smiles.

"Izzy, please, or Ma. Ma works too," Ma tells her.

I shake my head, biting my lip, and get another squeeze from Rebel's hand.

"You're very kind, Izzy. I'll think about it. I didn't expect any of this, and I'm sure Rocco doesn't want me around his family all the time."

"Stay, Rebel," I tell her, hating the idea of her moving around, especially with Beau somewhere out there and not knowing if he has any ideas of coming after her or the kid. "At least until we know about..."

"You can stay with me. I'm in the market for a new roommate," Trace adds with a smug grin on his face, only getting in the conversation to piss me off.

"She has a place with me," I tell him as my lips curl on the last word.

"If you say so, brother." He smirks.

"New topic," Ma says, stopping me from bringing up Beau. "Adaline, do you want to color some more?"

"Yes!" Adaline screeches.

"Maybe after dessert, we can do it together. Would you like that, sweetie?" Ma smiles down the table, and her eyes move to me. She's making moves for me, and no matter what she says, there's no denying it.

Adaline's eyes are so damn big. "Really?"

"I've always wanted a little girl around to draw with me."

"Let's go now," Adaline says, shoving one more spoonful of whipped cream into her mouth before leaping out of Rebel's lap.

My mother slides out of her seat before Adaline makes it to her. "You guys enjoy. We girls are going to color."

"And so it begins," I mutter, shaking my head.

If my mother has her way, Rebel will never leave. And if I'm being honest with myself, I'd be okay with it too.

But is it because I still have feelings for Rebel, or is it the tragedy of that day that draws me to her?

12

REBEL

THE MEN HAVE GONE OUTSIDE, AND ADALINE FOLLOWED them, leaving his mother and me alone for the very first time.

"Come sit." Rocco's mother pats the couch cushion next to her.

I tuck a lock of hair behind my ear as I move toward her, praying her lovely behavior wasn't just a ruse she played out in front of her boys.

My bottom barely makes contact when she starts to speak again. "How are you really doing?" she asks, studying my face with her mesmerizing blue eyes.

"I'm well," I lie, swallowing immediately but somehow plastering a smile on my face.

She tilts her head, continuing her appraisal as she moves her eyes across my features before connecting with my gaze again. "I see a lot of me in you. The tough façade. The tamped-down emotions. As women, we sometimes feel we have to portray strength even when our insides feel anything but." She reaches forward, taking my hand in hers. "I don't know everything you went through, but Carmello's told me enough for me to know you're in the right place."

"I..." My words die in my throat, along with the fake smile I've somehow maintained until now.

What do I say to something like that?

First, I make a mental note to kick Carmello in the balls. He talks more than any girl I know. Chatty Cathy's going to be his new nickname from this day forward. Second, Rocco told Carmello, so he's on my shit list at least a little bit too.

She squeezes my hand lightly. "The men in this family are extremely protective, Rebel. If you're in trouble, they will make it their mission to keep you and that sweet baby girl of yours safe. A woman with such pride and strength as you have wants to push against it, but don't. Don't fight it. Don't push away the help. I see the fire burning in your eyes. You think you need no one, especially not the protection of a man, after everything you've been through, but this is the time you lean into it instead of pulling away."

I gawk at her for a few seconds, blinking, and let her words settle. "It's not easy, Mrs. Caldo."

She raises an eyebrow.

"Izzy." I smile genuinely.

"I was the same way when I met James. I thought I didn't need anyone at my side to protect me or to lean on. I grew up with four brothers..."

My eyes widen. "Four brothers?"

She nods with a small laugh. "They're still a pain in my ass, even after all these years."

"I always wanted a brother," I admit.

Her face softens. "I complain about them a lot, but my life wouldn't be as full without them. They taught me early how to take care of and protect myself. For a long time, I thought that was enough, and then I met James and he blew that out of the water."

"I've never had anyone to lean on. I learned, at an early age, no one would look out for me except me. Then the accident happened." My gaze dips, and I take a deep breath, but I keep going when she tightens her hold on my hand still clutched in hers. "I'd hoped Beau was going to be my saving grace."

"Was he always bad?"

I lift my head with a slight shake. "No. He was wonderful for a little while. Everything I ever dreamed of. He was attentive and loving, but then he changed and…"

She scoots closer to me and slides her hand up my arm until it is on my shoulder. "You can stop running. You have us."

My nose tingles, and I blink away the water pooling in my eyes. The sentiment is as sweet as the woman sitting in front of me, but how can I ask a man I've spent so little time with to deal with the bullshit I created? "Rocco and Carmello are making it pretty damn hard for me to run from them at this point."

She chuckles. "My boys are a bit much."

"Ya think?" I laugh too.

"Take this time to regroup and figure out your next move. You can do it without someone watching or breathing down your neck. There's no urgency to move on. A child needs stability as much as they need love, Rebel. You can't be running from city to city to avoid your ex. Let the men figure things out while you get your plan together. Promise me you won't run."

"I promise. I only want what's best for Adaline."

She smiles warmly and moves her hand to my face like we've known each other forever. "Don't forget about yourself in the process. Children can feel our emotions, no matter how hard we try to hide from them. They're little sponges, soaking up the good with the bad. She seems happy right now." Izzy gazes out of the window behind the couch, and my eyes follow the sound of laughter. "She looks happy too."

Rocco and Carmello are chasing Adaline around the backyard as she squeals with her arms flailing about. I haven't seen such joy on her face in ages, and it warms my insides.

"On Sunday, the entire family is getting together for dinner as we do every week. I'd love for you and Adaline to come. There will be other kids there for her to play with too. She'd enjoy it, and I think you'd better understand my boys if you met the other pain-in-the-ass men in my family too."

Weekly family dinners? I don't even know what to say or do with that. I have no family besides my miserable aunt who wrote me off the day I graduated from high school. We never had dinner together. We never had anything together except misery.

"Wouldn't that be weird, though?" I ask, glancing her way as she stares out the window at her boys and Adaline with a big smile on her face. "I mean, I'm not family."

Her blue eyes move back to mine. "Family is more than blood. It'll be good for you and Adaline. Plus, my mom makes the best food you'll ever eat. And..." she says, moving her head back toward the boys and Adaline outside, "I don't think Rocco will be comfortable leaving you at home alone. Not yet, at least. Come for his peace of mind if nothing else, or at least the homemade sauce and meatballs."

"We'll go if Rocco wants us to," I reply, leaving an out just in case. It's great for his mother to ask me, but until I hear the words from his mouth, I can't guarantee I'll just tag along.

She smiles as her hand drops back to mine, and she gives the top a quick pat. "He'll ask."

The lamp on the side table casts a soft glow on her face. She's completely and absolutely stunning. The boys have a few of her features, but they look more like their father, who is hot as fuck for an older man. Their wide bodies, broad shoulders, and the strong jawlines all clearly come from him.

Adaline runs into the house, giggling and gasping for air with Rocco right on her heels. She doesn't make it to me before he leans forward, scooping her into the air and turning in a circle, only making her scream louder.

"Ready, babe? We should get home," he asks, still holding Adaline in his arms and moving her around like she's her own personal airplane.

My belly flutters with his words. I like the sound of them coming out of his mouth way too much.

"Yeah," I answer, tamping down the butterflies that have no place being inside my body.

The man is just being nice.

"You can stay a little while longer," his mother offers, standing from the couch and moving toward Rocco and Adaline. "It's been wonderful to hear the sound of laughter in the house again."

"Ma," he warns, but he is smiling at her. "Come on."

"What?" she asks, looking innocent.

"The kid has to go to bed, and it's getting late."

"Where's Rocco, and what have you done with him?" she teases him as I watch in awe once again at the easy way they love each other.

"Babe," Rocco says again as I sit there, watching him and his mother, while he still has Adaline in his arms. "You ready or you stayin'?"

I move from the couch, finally finding my legs. "I'm ready."

"Bath and bed," he tells Adaline as she sits in his arms.

"Story," she negotiates with him, giving him big pouty eyes.

"Fine. One," he tells her because the guy is a sucker

for the kid, and she has gotten him wrapped around her little finger in under a day, and she damn well knows it too.

"Two," she replies.

He stares at her, and she stares right back.

"One."

"Three," she says, upping her game.

"Two."

She smiles and nods. "Two."

"Damn," he mutters, shaking his head.

"Walked right into it, big guy." I cover my mouth to hide my laughter.

Rocco leans forward, placing his hand on Adaline's back to keep her steady, and kisses his mother's cheek. "Thanks for dinner, Ma."

"See you Sunday, yeah?" she asks as soon as he backs away. "All three of you."

His eyes move to me, and mine widen. "You good with that?"

"I…uh… I guess, but only if you…"

"We'll be there," he tells her, but he winks at me. "Adaline will love having the other kids to play with."

"I'll let your grandmother know to expect two more for dinner," his mother tells him, brushing her fingers against Adaline's cheek. "Sleep well, baby girl. See you at dinner, yeah?"

"Bye," Adaline says, moving into her touch like they've been doing this forever.

Adaline loves so easy and so fast. That's the thing about kids.

Before making it to the door, I stop and place my arms around Rocco's mother. "Thank you for everything."

She squeezes me, making me feel so many emotions, ones I've never felt so quickly. "You're welcome, Rebel. It was wonderful to have two more girls under my roof. I hope it's not the only time. Don't make yourself a stranger."

"I won't. I promise." I pull away from her slowly, loving the way the entire family loves.

"If you need a sitter—"

"Ma," Rocco interrupts her. "If we need a sitter, you're the first person we'll call."

"Good." His mother nods. "Sleep well," she tells Adaline and gets a giggle in response.

I follow Rocco out as he carries Adaline, holding her by the waistband of her pants and letting her pretend she's a bird flying through the air. Her arms are extended and flapping as he lifts and dips her in dramatic fashion.

"You're going to make her throw up," I warn him.

"She's good," he tells me. "Relax."

"Your funeral." I shrug.

As he lifts her, straightening her body to put her in the SUV, her mouth opens, and every ounce of whipped cream, ice cream, and apple pie flies out, splattering on the ground near Rocco's feet, barely missing his leg.

He tips his head down, blinking at the puddle of the remnants of dessert near his boots. "Fuck," he hisses, but he's not mad. Surprised, yeah, but mad...no.

"Told you," I say, giggling.

His gaze snaps to me, and I cover my mouth, trying to kill my laughter. "Could've been worse," he says easily before turning his attention to Adaline. "You okay, kid?" He swipes his thumb across her chin and lip, capturing the little bit that is left behind.

She nods but is barely moving. "Sorry," she whispers.

His face softens as he smiles at her. "Not the first time a chick has puked on me. Probably won't be the last," he tells her, to which I roll my eyes.

"You're not mad?" she asks.

"No, baby. I'm not mad. Ready to get home and read a story?"

"Two," she reminds him as he places her in her car seat.

"Mind like a steel trap. It's genetic."

"What?" I ask, moving to the passenger side door.

"Women."

I stand by the door, watching him as he buckles her in carefully and gently. "What about us?"

"Even at a young age, you forget nothing."

"It's a gift."

He ticks his head toward the front seat. "Ass inside, Reb."

"Bossy much?" I reply but do as I'm told anyway.

He is bossy, but not in the way that pisses me off. For some reason, the words sounded sweet, although they were short and gruff.

"Let's get the princess home and tucked in," he tells her before closing the door.

"Mommy," Adaline calls out from the back seat while Rocco walks around the SUV.

I turn to look into her cute little face. "Yeah, baby?"

"I like him," she says, smiling at me.

"Me too, baby. Me too," I say honestly, returning her sweet smile.

13

ROCCO

THE KID SMELLS LIKE STRAWBERRIES WHEN SHE CLIMBS up on my bed and snuggles into my side with a book in her hands.

One book.

Not two, but one.

She places her head on my shoulder and stares up at me with those big blue eyes. "Ready," she whispers, pushing the book in my face.

"You don't have to do this," Rebel says from the doorway, watching us.

"We're fine. Come back in ten," I tell her.

"Twenty," Adaline insists. "Not ten."

"Twenty what?" I ask, peering down at her, and I wonder if she even has a clue what we're talking about.

"Minutes." She smiles.

I'm a total goner between this little girl's smarts and beauty.

How in the world can any man turn his back on

someone as sweet and pure as her? When she looks at me with those blue eyes, I'll move heaven and earth to see the smile on her face and keep the pain away.

"Fifteen," I tell Rebel, meeting Adaline in the middle.

Adaline yawns and I know she doesn't even have ten in her, but I'll give her a few more minutes to make her happy.

"I'm going to jump in the shower. Is that okay?" Rebel asks me.

"Sugar, do whatever you want to do. Take a bath. It's way better."

She stares at me for a moment, biting her lip. "I don't know…"

"Lots of bubbles," I tell her and wrap my arm around the kid as she gets restless at my side. "Take your time. I got this."

"Okay," she says, walking into the room and leaning over Adaline. "Night, baby." She kisses Adaline's cheek, peeking up at me. "You too."

I wink at her. "Enjoy your bath."

She gazes at me for a moment, her cheeks turning pink, before she turns around, stalking out of the room quicker than she entered.

"Story," Adaline says, tapping on the hard cover with her pudgy little index finger.

"What's this one about?" I lift up the book and study the cover, spotting the girls with their frilly dresses, and somehow hold in my groan. "Princesses."

Adaline cuddles closer, running her finger over my

T-shirt as she stares at the first page. She's a captive audience as I read.

She barely moves, and she's paying careful attention with each passing page. The book is ridiculously short, with twenty pages that have no more than a few sentences each.

"The end," I say, closing the book when I reach the final page.

"More," is her immediate response.

I peer down at her, and she doesn't even look remotely tired, but I am. "Do you have another book?"

She shakes her head. "I'll tell you a story," she says.

What the hell? Why not? I wouldn't even know where to begin with telling her a story out of thin air. I've crafted some crazy shit in my days, but they were mostly lies to cover my ass and nowhere near a bedtime story unless I had a stripper snuggled in my arms.

"Sure, kid. Tell me a story." I smile down at her, and she smiles back, making my heart squeeze with her cuteness.

"Once upon a time," she says, repeating the same words from the start of the story I just finished, "there was a cow…"

I close my eyes, letting her babble on about a cow and a horse. I have no idea what's going on or what she's talking about, but she goes on and on and on. I cover my mouth to hide my yawn.

"Are you listening?" Adaline asks.

"I am."

"Okay. So, the cow…"

I tune out again, thinking about Rebel in the next room, the sound of the water soothing.

I'm comfortable. More comfortable and content than I've been in a while.

The house is no longer quiet but filled with a little girl's voice and the soft whispers of Rebel as she sings to herself in the shower.

"Rocco." Rebel's soft voice echoes. "Rocco, wake up."

My eyes snap open. "Shit," I whisper.

Rebel puts her finger against her lips before pointing at Adaline, still snuggled against me and fast asleep. "Move slowly," she tells me.

At least this time, I have clothes on. I can't believe I fell asleep while Adaline told me a story, when I was supposed to be doing that very thing.

Epic adult fail, Rocco.

Way to go.

I slide to the side, almost falling to the floor before climbing to my feet. Rebel grabs my hand, pulling me from the bedroom.

"Thirsty?" I ask her, not ready to say good night and finding my second wind.

She nods, following me toward the kitchen. "Did she tell you one of her stories?"

I laugh. "She did."

"She's a pro." Rebel slides onto the stool at the island and pulls the rubber band from her hair, letting the strands flow freely. "Don't feel bad. She's put me to sleep more than once."

In the dim overhead lighting of the kitchen, Rebel's more beautiful than ever. Whatever bad shit has happened to her since the last time we saw each other, it hasn't diminished her natural glow.

My eyes linger a little too long on her cleavage that's clearly visible from the V-neck of the T-shirt she's wearing. "Water or something stronger?"

"You got a beer?" she asks, peering over my shoulder toward the fridge. "I could use one after that hot shower."

I grab two beers, twisting off the caps, and place one in front of her. "I thought I told you to take a bath, babe."

She takes a swig and slouches. "I wanted a shower. I didn't want to be in there all night."

"There's no rush here. You want to lie in the bath for an hour, you lie in the bath for an hour."

"Rocco," she says, shaking her head with a slight roll of her eyes. "When you have a child, you don't get to do things like lie in the bath for an hour, no matter how much you may want to."

I lean over the counter, my elbow propped and holding the beer as I rest my other hand near hers. "You're not the only adult here. I'm more than capable of watching the kid so you can take that hour-long bath."

Rebel glances down to where our hands are almost touching before bringing her gaze back to mine. "She's not your problem or responsibility. I'd never ask you to do that."

Inching my hand over, I touch her pinkie finger with mine. "Babe." I smile, cocking my head and staring her straight in the eyes. "You're in my house. My kid or not, you want a bath, she becomes my responsibility. The kid is the furthest thing from a problem. And for that matter, you're in my house, sleeping under my roof, you're my responsibility too."

She blinks a few times, eyebrows drawn in. "Hardly."

I place my beer on the countertop and round the island until I'm next to her. She stays still, staring straight ahead, beer in her hand.

"Rebel, look at me, sugar." When she doesn't do as I ask, I lift my hand to her face, touching her chin, and guide her gaze to mine.

"What?" she asks defiantly, chin up but eyes not on me.

"Eyes. I need your eyes."

I wait, not speaking, but I keep my fingers on her chin and our bodies connected. Slowly, she moves her pretty blue eyes to mine, and they're filled with fire.

Leaning forward, I bring my face within inches of hers but keep our eyes locked. "You ever let that tough shell fall away?"

Her gaze searches mine, and her breathing is shallow and fast. When she turns her body toward me, I know there's some hope.

"I don't have a shell anymore, Rocco. It was crushed a long time ago."

Flattening my palm, I slide my hand to her neck and

pull her up and toward me until our lips are almost touching. "The shell's there, babe. Harder than it's ever been, but that's fine. I'll work around it and slowly crack it open."

"Why would you do that?" she whispers against my lips. "We're not here to stay. We're temporary. Nothing but a small bump in your daily life before you're back where you were before you took us in off the street."

I tighten my fingers. "I didn't take you in off the street. I know you're tough as steel and could've made it on your own. But we had something once. Something great. Something hot. Something worth pursuing."

"It was a long time ago."

"It was." My thumb brushes the line of her jaw as I stare at her mouth, noticing the v on the top of her lip and wanting nothing more than to taste it. "But we never got to explore what it could be. It burned hot and bright before being snuffed out by what happened. We never got to explore what could've been, and I'm telling you now, with you sitting in my kitchen, drinking a beer, shooting the shit with me—I want to explore that."

She places her hand on my chest, the heat of her palm almost burning the skin underneath. "I have a child."

"And?" I whisper, moving between her legs and leaving no room between our bodies.

"I can't just jump back into your bed for fun. My responsibilities outweigh my need for you."

"You need me?" I ask, moving my other hand to her other cheek, cradling her face in my palms. "You want me, don't you? Say you want me as much as I want you."

She stares at me for a few seconds without blinking. Her eyes search mine like she's trying to find something there. Some reason to say no, even if I can see that same burning ember hidden in her blue depths that I feel simmering deep in my soul. "I do," she says with a swallow. "But…"

"No buts." I pull her face toward me. "I won't hurt you," I promise. "I'd never hurt you."

"Everyone hurts me," she whispers. "At some point, everyone in my life has hurt me."

I'm included in that lot. She called, and I didn't answer. She reached out, and I did nothing to extend a hand to her. I failed her like everyone else before.

"Baby, you fell into my life again, and this time, I'm not going to let anything take you away."

Her fingers curl into the material of my T-shirt. "You don't know what you're saying."

Her pulse quickens under my palm, matching my own. "I know exactly what I'm saying. Been years since I've kissed those lips. Years I've been tortured by what happened that weekend and what I lost. Not just how my heart broke, but the way we ended, snuffed out in an instant. You came back. You're here. I want you here, and nothing's going to change that. For the first time in a long time, my world doesn't seem so lonely. Everything feels right for once."

"We shouldn't," she whispers, her blue eyes pinned to mine.

"Tell me you don't feel the burn, and I'll stop."

"I…" She sucks in a breath, and for a second, I think she's going to push me away, but she doesn't. She tightens her fingers, twisting my shirt before she pulls me forward. "I need you."

I don't waste another moment before crashing my lips down on hers, tasting the cool sweetness of her lips. The memories, the feelings, the familiar way our mouths fit together comes back in one single touch. Everything else falls away as I pull her to me, holding her face still to feast on the delicate lines of her mouth.

She kisses me back, opening her lips as my tongue swipes across the bottom one. The softness of her moans isn't lost on me as she wraps her arms over and around my shoulders, tipping her head back to give me more access.

Diving deeper, I take everything Rebel's offering. Her hands slide to my hair, running over the short strands in the back and holding my face to hers. But I'm not going anywhere. The same fire that burned bright ten years ago is no longer a flicker but a full-blown flame.

"Put your legs around me," I tell her between kisses when I finally come up for air.

She doesn't even hesitate before complying, wrapping those long legs around my waist. I slide my hands to her bottom, lifting her from the stool and depositing her on the countertop.

Our hands roam freely as our kisses become frantic and erratic. Her hand slips underneath the hem of my T-shirt, her skin making contact with mine, lighting the fuse.

My mouth leaves hers, gliding down her neck, relishing the softness of her skin against my lips until I find the swell of her breasts. She gasps as my mouth touches her sensitive flesh, and my hand finds its way under her shirt. My finger strokes the edge of her lacy bra as I kiss my way across her cleavage.

Her legs tighten around me, her middle grinding against mine.

Fuck.

She feels so good in my arms. Like everything I remember, but better. The fantasy I've had for the last ten years is finally about to become reality.

I stare into her eyes, panting from need. "You want it gentle?"

"No," she rasps, hunger flashing in her eyes. "Fuck me hard, baby. Own me," she breathes.

TRACE'S eyes are the first ones on me as I step through the door at Inked. "Nice look." He smirks.

"Don't be a shithead," I growl, lifting my coffee to my lips, needing the caffeine.

He sets down his pencil on top of his sketch and leans back in his chair, eyes on me. "Not being a shithead, asshole. You have a new decoration on your body you didn't have the last time I saw you."

I narrow my eyes, and his smile only widens. "What decoration?"

He points at me, wagging his finger toward my neck. "Hickey."

I roll my eyes. "You've had a million."

"I was a kid then, but you're a grown man and I remember you busting my balls a lot about it."

"That's what brothers do," I grumble.

"Finally got yourself a piece of the sweet stuff again, and you're still a miserable prick."

I take a deep breath, trying to relax, knowing I didn't get nearly as much sleep as I needed. "I'm tired, kid. Just tired."

"You're old, bro. Fuckin' ain't so easy at your age."

I glare at him. "You better watch yourself, kid."

He laughs. "Hey. At least your dick still works. That counts for something."

My brother Trace is a dick. He always has been a dick, and he's spoiled as fuck. That shit came with being the youngest and never having to share anything in his life. Mello and I were born together, never knowing what it was like to be a single, but Trace reveled in it.

I collapse into the chair next to his station, the rest of the place still empty. "You act like I'm ancient."

He cocks his head, lips flat, eyebrow raised. "Most of the time, you act like you have one foot in the grave. Like you said...fucking ancient."

I shake my head and put my feet up on my stool, ready to school my brother in the ways of life. "My life hasn't been like yours—"

"Save your tragedy, bro. You're alive. You're not too bad-looking. You are kind of young when you're not acting old, which isn't often, and you have the chick you've been pining over for years lying in your bed. Get your head out of your ass and put a smile on that face. Life is looking up."

I blink, staring at him, soaking in all the words he just vomited. He wasn't wrong about some things. I do have what I wanted, but keeping it is going to be the problem.

"You know nothing about love or women," I tell him.

He crosses his arms over his chest, smiling. "I get more pussy than you do. Trust me on that one. I know plenty about women, and I know all about you, big brother. If you're not careful, you're going to lose this one. She'll be your greatest mistake."

I scrub my hand down my face. "I got this. I know what I'm doing. I let her go once. I'm not going to let it happen again."

He raises an eyebrow. "You sure about that?"

"Dead fucking serious."

He smiles. "Good. It'll get Ma off my ass about settling down and having kids. I need you and Mello to get your shit together so I can enjoy the next decade or so."

"Sorry we're late," Gigi says, rushing through the front door, her hair a wild mess. "We were, uh…"

"Fucking," Trace finishes her sentence.

She stops dead, glaring at him. "What? No. We weren't fucking."

Trace points at her head. "Your hair says otherwise."

Gigi groans, lifting her hand to her hair and trying to smooth it. "Goddamn bike. I hate those freaking helmets."

"Helmet head is better than dead head, darlin'," Pike says, coming in after her.

"Whatever," she mutters, dropping her purse next to her station like she always does. "I heard you had a nice time last night, Roc."

"It was okay," I lie. It was the best.

"Your mom seemed really happy."

"You talked to her?" I ask, sitting up a little straighter.

"She called me this morning about the AC tech coming to check out the unit and told me you, Rebel, and her little girl were over for dinner. Aunt Izzy sounded over the moon."

"I'm sure," I mumble.

"She already has you married and preggers in her head."

"Fucking great."

Gigi bumps me with her hip. "It wouldn't be so bad. You'd be a great dad and husband."

I peer up at her like she's off her rocker. "You know me, right?"

"Yes," she says, slapping me on the shoulder. "You're protective, loyal, and sweet when you want to be. A girl like Rebel needs that."

"A girl like Rebel?"

"Dude." Gigi shakes her head, rolling her eyes. "You told me all about her once when you were drunk. You went on and on about her shit life. I thought you'd cave in the last ten years and pick up the phone, going after that sweet pussy—your words, not mine—you couldn't shake."

"She's more than pussy, Gigi."

She smirks. "I know, fool. You're hooked. Gone. Done for. Might as well buy the ring now and get it over with."

"She said she isn't sticking around."

"She wants you to chase, Rocco. She needs to know you're going to stick. She's had enough bad. She wants to know the good is going to be there always before she'll let her guard down. You give her all of yourself, and she'll be yours forever."

"Maybe."

"Fuck her yet?" Gigi asks, waiting at my side.

"I don't kiss and tell."

She laughs. "Cousin, you do. You so fucking do. Want me to start naming all the pussy you've had and how you had it?"

"Nope."

"You lock that shit down, and you lock it down tight," Pike tells me, adding his two cents to this incredibly awkward conversation.

"Working on it."

"What are we talking about?" That question comes

from Lily as she strolls into the room, looking fresh and sweet.

I don't know how she does it. The woman is put together, put together. Kids didn't change that either.

"Rocco and Rebel."

"Just the combo is sexy and meant to be."

I shake my head. "You're all nuts."

Lily gets closer, leaning over into my space. "Do you have a hickey?"

My hand moves to my neck, covering the spot I remember Rebel sucking on last night. "Shut it," I tell her.

She smiles, giving me a wink. "Good job, big guy. You moved on her faster than I thought you would." Her long, thin finger pokes my chest. "Glad to know there's still a heart in there somewhere."

I growl, but man, I love my cousin. She's everything sweet and good. It's almost impossible to be mean to her because she's just that nice. "I'm doing what I can, Lily. I'll try not to fuck it up."

"Good." Her smile widens. "Your ma has a lot riding on this one."

"You too?" I groan.

"She called early while I was making breakfast. We chatted. She told me what happened and how happy she was for you."

"We all need to back up a little," I say those words to everyone. "It's been a decade since Rebel and I were together. We're still feeling each other out."

"And from the looks of it, that's going well," Lily teases me.

"I've got shit to do," I say, standing and heading toward the stock room.

"Add Rebel to that list," Trace calls out, earning a middle finger high in the air and over my shoulder.

"He's so done and doesn't even know it," Gigi says to them. "About fucking time."

I can't even be mad.

They've been through it all with me.

They know my bullshit.

They also know I have, indeed, been pining for the girl who's haunted my dreams for years.

After Rebel and Adaline are safe, I'll do whatever I have to do to make them mine.

14

REBEL

I STAND IN THE MIDDLE OF THE KITCHEN, STARING AT what feels like an endless sea of people. They welcomed Adaline and me, saying hello, and each and every one of them hugged me.

They hugged me…

We were strangers to them, and yet they opened their arms to us, doing everything possible to make us feel wanted.

Is this what it is like to have a family? Unconditional love and acceptance, something I never knew or believed with the way I grew up.

A small woman with gray hair grabs on to Rocco's arm, studying me. "Welcome to my home," she says to me. "I hope you brought your appetite, honey. We eat in this household."

I give her a smile, knowing I could gain a few pounds, but food isn't a priority when your life is falling apart around you. "I love to eat, ma'am, and from what I hear, you make the best food in town."

A little girl runs up to Adaline and grabs on to her hand. "Want to play?" she asks her, not even questioning who she is or why she's here.

Adaline tips her head back, peering up at me. "Mommy, can I? Please."

I give her a quick nod, and she takes off with the little girl without a moment's hesitation.

"That's Avery, my cousin Nick's little girl, and Adaline will be fine," Rocco tells me, giving my hand a light squeeze as I watch them disappear. "Let her go. She'll have more fun with her and can meet everyone later."

I tip my head up, staring into his dark-brown eyes, feeling the butterflies that took up residence inside my belly yesterday fluttering once again. "I'm okay," I reassure him.

He leans over, placing his mouth next to my ear. "Breathe, sugar. I know this is a lot for you, but everyone here is family, and they're going to treat you as such. Don't get freaked out."

"I'm not freaked out," I lie, plastering a smile on my face.

"Good," the woman at his side says. "I'm Grandma, but you can call me Gram or Nonna. Those are your only two options. No ma'am or Mrs. Gallo. When you're at my house, eating my food, and on the arm of my grandson, you're one of us."

"Your favorite grandson," Rocco adds, winking at

the small woman who's solely responsible for all the people inside this house.

"Always." The woman beams, but I have a feeling she feeds the same line to every grandkid. "I better go check the sauce. It needs my final tweaks. Have a glass of wine and settle in, sweetie. This is a marathon, not a sprint."

I don't know what that means, but I could take a little less running in my life. I'm mentally and physically exhausted. But after the last few days, I don't feel so weighed down by the things I've been running from.

"Rebel," Izzy, Rocco's mom, calls out, walking toward us with her arms open. "I'm so happy you came."

"Thank you," I tell her as I hug her back, feeling all kinds of things from the outpouring of love and acceptance.

"Rocco," she says, still holding on to me. "Your father wants to talk to you in your grandfather's study."

"Reb, are you—"

"She'll be fine," Izzy tells him. "Let us ladies have some time together. I'll introduce her to everyone. You know how your father doesn't like to be kept waiting. Tommy's in there too."

"Oh boy," Rocco mutters.

I pull away from Izzy's embrace, seeing Rocco hasn't moved an inch. "Go. I'll be fine."

He studies me for a second before he peels away, walking toward the other room.

"He's a protective thing, isn't he?" Izzy whispers,

taking my arm and guiding me away before I have a chance to answer. "Remember my brothers I told you about?"

"Yeah." I smile, looking through the crowd, trying to figure out which males could be her siblings. It's quick and easy to pick them out, with the same intense eyes and no-nonsense air about them.

"My brother Thomas is with James right now. You'll meet him later," she says as we stop at the entrance to the living room. She points to a wide-shouldered man, sitting with a blond woman between his legs. "That's Joe. He looks cranky as fuck, but trust me, he's a kitten."

My eyebrows rise. "Doesn't look like it," I whisper, but I watch the way he runs his fingers down his wife's arm like the attention he pays her is natural and not forced.

"Oh, he has a side to him. But trust me, he loves deep and would jump in front of a bullet for anyone in this family."

Well, okay. I've never been able to say the same about anyone. I'm pretty fucking sure my aunt would've pushed me in front of that bullet in order to save herself. I can't imagine what it feels like to be so important someone else would give their life for yours.

I feel that way about Adaline. I'd walk through fire to save her life. I'd do anything, suffer any fate, as long as she'd have a happy life. I want to give her everything I never had but always wanted.

But these people…they have it. They probably don't know how lucky they are either.

"Joe is our best artist at Inked, but like me, he's about ready to retire and hand over the entire operation to the kids." She tightens her arm as she pulls me closer. "That's his wife, Suzy, between his legs. Girl couldn't even say the word 'shit' when they met, but now…" Izzy laughs, shaking her head. "Let's just say loving a man like my brother has a way of changing a woman."

I can see that about him. Joe is spectacularly handsome. Rugged and chiseled jaw, with the perfect smattering of salt-n-pepper hair, blue eyes, and covered in tattoos. Even at his age, he could probably talk just about any woman into bending over and touching her toes for a taste.

"Joe and Suzy have three girls—Gigi, Luna, and Rosie—who are outside, no doubt gossiping out of earshot. You'll meet them and Rocco's other cousins in a bit."

Izzy points to another man stretched out on the floor, back against a chair, woman between his legs too. I sense a theme, and it isn't the women waiting on the men. "That's Mike. He used to be a big shot fighter, then he found Mia, who's a doctor. She didn't have the stomach for the blood, so he gave it up right after he won his first championship."

"No shit," I whisper.

"No shit," she repeats. "They have a son named Stone, a daughter named Lily, and her husband's Jett."

Mike is bigger than Joe but just as impressive. But

the things that keep drawing my eye aren't their handsome faces, but the way they cling to their women as if they worship them and never want to be without their hands on them.

"That's Anthony and Max," Izzy says, ticking her head toward the other side of the room to a couple who are also snuggled up, staring at a phone and laughing about something. "They're Tamara and Asher's parents. Anthony also works at Inked, but he's about to hang up his tattoo gun to finally enjoy being a grandfather."

"That's sweet."

"Yeah. Must be nice to have children who have given you babies," she says with a salty tone, and I know she's talking about her three boys and their unsettled lifestyle. "I'm the only one who isn't a grandmother here."

"I'm sorry," I tell her, feeling a bit awkward but also sorry for her too. The woman clearly loves family. Cherishes it even, but her boys haven't delivered on the thing she seems to want the most. "Maybe soon."

She turns her face toward me and smiles. "I'm counting on it."

My belly flutters again, and I don't think she's talking in generalizations, but looking at me as the possible pot of gold at the end of the grandchild rainbow.

A beautiful redhead walks through the crowd, making her way toward us. Her smile is electrifying and sweet, easily sucking someone in. "Hi, Rebel. I'm Angel," she says, extending her hand to me.

As soon as I take it, she pulls me in, hugging me. "It's so nice to finally meet you."

Finally? I've been here only a few days, and word has spread far and wide enough for people to know about me.

"Thanks," I say, but it comes out more like a question.

"Angel and I talk daily. Our husbands, my brother Thomas and my husband James, own a security company together. She keeps me clued in on the shit the guys would rather we be clued out about."

Angel laughs as she releases me. "I always got your back, sis. Gotta keep those men on their toes."

"James sure as fuck keeps me on mine," Izzy replies with a hint of laughter.

"You like it, you dirty bitch. Don't pretend otherwise."

"Hey," Izzy says, tilting her head. "Don't act all prim and proper. I seem to remember hearing about a time you slapped my brother and—"

Angel's eyes flash, and her face reddens. "Do you want to help in the kitchen, Rebel?"

"She's a guest," Izzy reminds her sister-in-law. "Are you changing the subject, Angel baby?"

"We all have our kinks, Iz." Angel smirks, crossing her arms in front of her chest and staring back at Izzy. "I mean, I've never kneeled at Thomas's feet before."

Izzy throws her head back and laughs. "Sweetie, don't pretend you haven't been on your knees before.

We may have a different style, but the ending is always the same."

My mouth's hanging open at the way they're talking to each other, but I guess this is how sisters talk when there's no filter or secrets.

"Izzy's a sub," Angel tells me.

I blink, confused. "She's a sandwich?" I ask, getting two weird looks in return.

Izzy looks at Angel, and Angel stares at her, staying silent for a moment before they burst into laughter.

"Funniest shit ever," Izzy says, almost unable to get the words out because she's laughing so hard, she can barely speak.

"Sandwich," Angel chuckles, touching my arm. "Oh, darling. You have so much to learn."

"So...not a sandwich. Got it." I'm wondering what I'm missing, but I'm not about to ask.

"Anyway..." Izzy guides me toward what I assume is the kitchen since Angel's right behind us. "Come hang out with us for a little bit until Rocco's done with his father. We could always use an extra hand since we're feeding a small army."

"I can see that," I tell her, still taking in the people she hasn't pointed out to me.

A hand comes out, grabbing me gently by the wrist and stopping us. "And who do we have here?" the man with the white beard asks, giving me a soft and warm smile.

"Bear, this is Rocco's girl, Rebel," Izzy explains and

points a finger at him. "And I expect you to behave around her."

He releases me and lifts his hands in the air, but there's an unmistakable smirk on his face. "Hey, now. I always behave, sweetness."

Izzy drops her hip. "You never behave. You and Aunt Fran are the worst."

Bear swipes his hand in the air. "Ignore her," he tells me, not looking at Izzy anymore. "So, you're Rocco's girl. It's fucking fabulous to finally meet you."

"Um," I mutter and bite the corner of my lip, thinking I'm missing a fucking lot. "I'm just an old friend. Not his girl."

Am I his girl? We have history, and the last couple of nights were off-the-charts hot just like it was ten years ago. It was like time didn't exist or matter, and we picked up right where we left off.

Bear runs his hand through his beard, studying me and making me feel naked. "Beautiful but clueless."

I blink and stiffen. "Excuse me?"

"Heard your name come out of his mouth before, darlin'."

"Bear," Izzy warns.

"What, sweetness? Just stating the obvious. Rocco doesn't bring 'friends' here for dinner. Hell, he's never brought anyone here for family dinner. The girl can keep believing she's a friend or start settling into the fact she's taken and doesn't know it."

"Izzy invited me," I correct him. "I assure you we're only friends."

He gives me a shit-eating grin. "Sure, beautiful. Whatever makes your path forward easier to travel."

"Ignore him," Izzy says, pulling me away from the rough-looking man who only spoke sweet words, although ones that threw me totally off track. "He's a bit off."

"Is he?"

She nods, smiling.

"That's so sad," I whisper.

Angel smacks Izzy's arm. "Bear isn't off. Stop acting like he has dementia."

"I didn't say he had dementia. I said he was off, as in a little crazy. You work with him every day. You know how he is."

"He's sharp as can be, especially given his age. He just calls it like he sees it," Angel says, and I suddenly wonder if I've stepped into something more than I imagined.

"There she is," Rocco's grandmother says as soon as she sees us and before I have a chance to ask anything else about Bear's comments. "You want to help, honey? I could use an extra pair of hands."

She's so sweet, how can I possibly say no? "I'd love to help, ma'am—" She gives me a look, and I instantly realize my mistake. "Nonna."

Her face breaks out into a big smile. "Perfect, child. Now, go wash up. You're going to be rolling a lot of balls."

"Gram," Carmello says, walking into the kitchen behind me. "Can you please not call them balls?"

She stares at him, lips flat, not amused. "If you can't hang without thinking about what's between your legs, then shoo, boy, shoo. Not everything is about your dick."

I rock back, shocked to hear her say dick so casually. I love this family. They are all kinds of crazy, but in that fun way that could suck you in, soaking deep into your soul.

Carmello grumbles and comes to stand next to me at the sink. "Hey, Reb." He leans against the counter, crossing his arms, facing the opposite direction. "You doin' okay? Rocco being a grumpy asshole?"

I scrub my hands together but give Carmello my eyes. "He's been really great with Adaline, and we're doing okay. Getting along just fine."

I'm being evasive, but this is Carmello, and the one thing I've learned about him is he can't keep a secret, especially from his mother.

"Good." He nods, leaning a little closer. "He needs someone to unwind him. I think you're just the person to do it too."

I lean his way, dropping my voice so only he can hear me over the chatter of the women in the background. "I'm not his saving grace, Carm. I'm just a girl, passing through."

"You're not just a girl. You're *the* girl."

I blink again, my hands still under the water, but I'm no longer scrubbing them. "I'm not *the* girl." I pause, and he stares at me, raising an eyebrow. I gasp, covering my mouth. "I can't be *the* girl, Carm. We barely know each other."

"So…" He lifts his hand to his face, running his fingers across his jaw. "You're saying you don't feel that way about him, then? Because if he's off base, you better tell him now before you guys—" he leans close, dropping his voice to a whisper "—do it again and he catches more feelings."

"He doesn't have feelings for me."

"Chick is fucking clueless," he mutters into the air, glancing up at the ceiling.

"I'm not clueless," I argue as I switch off the faucet and wipe my hands dry, staring him down when he's done talking to himself.

"Y'are, sweetheart. My brother doesn't open his house and life to just anyone."

I lean the side of my hip into the counter, the women in the room all talking and ignoring us…thankfully. "I'm sure your brother has had plenty of women over the last ten years."

He nods slowly, a smirk playing on his lips. "He's had women, but not the way you think. Rocco's had to overcome a lot of control issues. I don't have a right to out him and his kink."

I draw in my eyebrows. "Kink?"

He slides away, still smiling. "Talk to him yourself, Reb. You're in for more than you think, and I'm pretty fucking sure you're about to have your mind blown." He presses his hand to his chest, dipping his chin. "I just want you to know what you're in for if you decide he's *the* guy for you, too."

He walks away slowly, leaving me standing at the counter, confused and filled with so many more questions than answers.

15

ROCCO

"You need to tell her," Dad says as soon as Thomas leaves us alone in the study. He lifts his glass to his lips, staring at me over the rim. "About everything."

"I will." I rub my hands down and up my jeans, trying to stop my legs from shaking. "I just don't want to fuck this up."

"Want to know how to fuck it up for sure?"

"How?" I groan, knowing what he's going to say before he says it.

"By hiding shit from her."

I sigh. "You understand the need. I understand the craving. But…" I lean back, kicking out my leg. "What if she doesn't? Then what the hell do I do?"

My father takes a sip of his bourbon, studying me as he places the glass on his knee. "Kid, she'll either accept you for what and who you are, or she won't. The real question is, what are you going to do if she doesn't? Can you give it up? Can you change?"

"Fuck," I hiss, tipping my head back and closing my eyes for a few seconds. "Talking about this makes my skin crawl, but I gotta ask..." I bring my gaze back to him, needing to know the answer to questions I've never asked. "Was Mom into it when you met her?"

Dad shakes his head. "No. She sure as hell wasn't. We eased her into the lifestyle. When a man needs control, it's hard to give it up. But we didn't go to clubs for a while. I took a step back from that part of my life, but I made damn sure she knew who was in control in the bedroom."

Somehow, I stop myself from gagging. Talking to my parents about sex hasn't ever been comfortable. When I started to spiral down into a dark place after the accident, my dad stepped in, and I learned more about him than I ever wanted to know. We talked in general-izations, never bringing up his and my mother's rela-tionship. Now, I feel like I need to know more because Rebel is just as stubborn as my mother, and I find it hard to believe my father was ever able to make my mom kneel.

"Enough." I raise my hand, shifting in my seat, hunching over my legs with my elbows on my knees. "I'll talk to Rebel."

"Sooner rather than later, son. You need to tell her about Beau, too. It's important for a woman like her, someone who's had their trust broken and been emotionally and physically hurt by a man who was supposed to love her, to be with a man who's open, honest, protective, and caring. You need to put her needs above your own if you ever want a future with her."

"Am I crazy?" I ask.

"For what?"

"I can't describe how I feel around her. There's this inexplicable pull when she's around me. I felt it ten years ago, and it's stronger now."

"Rocco, I knew the moment I laid eyes on your mother. Knew it deep down in my soul. You feel how you feel, and there's no rhyme or reason to any of it. I just want you to go after whatever makes you happy."

"I haven't felt as much peace as I have in the last few days for over ten years, Dad. That means something."

He stands, placing his glass on the coffee table. "Talk to her. Do it today. Don't leave things unsaid. You'll either figure out how to move forward together or not, but either way, you'll have your answer." When he walks by me, he places his hand on my shoulder, giving me a tight squeeze. "Whatever you need, I'm always here. I'll always listen and do my best to guide you, son."

I touch his hand, squeezing it back as I glance up at him. "Thanks, Dad."

"Love you," he says softly.

"Love you too," I tell him before he walks out of the room, leaving me there to think about all the ways I could fuck everything up before it even really has a chance to start.

I TIPTOE out of Rebel's bedroom, not risking waking up Adaline after it took me three books to get her to fall asleep. The kid fought every yawn, twitching awake when her eyes would finally close.

When I walk into the living room, I find Rebel curled up underneath a blanket, a book in one hand and a glass of wine in the other. Her head comes up and she smiles, but she doesn't say a word.

She's been uncharacteristically quiet since we were at my grandmother's house. My family has a way of scaring some people off by nothing more than the sheer number of them. Then there's their mouths and the arguments about anything and everything that could be up for debate. I'm sure she was overwhelmed by all of it since she doesn't have family of her own.

I drop down onto the couch next to her, pulling her foot into my lap. "You okay?" I ask her.

"I'm fine," she says, peering up from her pages long enough to give me a smile. "Did Adaline give you any trouble?"

My fingers press into the bottom of her foot and her eyes flutter closed, but I keep contact. "Nah, sugar. Took a few books and she tried to tell me another story, but I didn't fall for it this time."

Rebel shuts her book, slouching down on the couch, poking her other foot out from underneath the blanket. "That's good," she breathes. "She seems to be comfortable around you."

"She's a great kid, but I'm more concerned about her mama."

"Today was overwhelming," she says softly.

"I can understand that. Sorry if my family was a bit much."

"You're really lucky, Rocco. All those people love you."

"I know I'm lucky. I was blessed being born into that group. Although sometimes, they can be a little crazy and a bit over the top."

"Pushy and not very subtle too," she adds with a smile. "Carmello talked to me for a bit when you were with your father."

I tighten my hands, rubbing her soles a little harder with my fingers. "What did he say?"

"That we had a lot to talk about." Rebel opens her eyes again, adjusting her body so she's sitting up, but her feet stay in my lap.

"Nosy fucker," I grunt. "He's right. We do have a lot to talk about. Come here, Reb. I want you closer."

"I'm pretty fucking close and comfortable too," she argues.

"In my lap, sugar. I want your eyes on mine when we talk."

She stares at me for a minute without speaking before moving across the couch and climbing on top of my lap. My hands find her hips, feeling at home there as she settles her weight against my lower half. Rebel snakes her arms around my shoulders, leaving very little

175

space between our bodies, but she gives me her blue eyes and full attention.

"I'm listening."

I lean back, keeping my hands on her hips and eyes locked on hers. "After the accident, I went to a dark place, Rebel."

"Me too," she admits. "Super dark. I'm lucky to be alive, and I probably wouldn't be if it weren't for Adaline."

I tighten my hands, giving her body a small squeeze. "When Carrie died in my arms, I felt powerless and had a lot of anger. My dad helped me, introduced me to something to help me feel like I had the power and control I thought had been taken from me."

"Okay," she murmurs as her fingers sweep through the back of my hair.

"I stopped dating after you. I had a taste, knew what I wanted and couldn't have, so I moved on to other ways to find pleasure, control, and some form of happiness without you in my life, sugar."

She blinks, staring at me with her eyebrows drawn inward. "I don't know what any of that means. Are you saying you haven't slept with another woman since you were with me?"

I pull her hips forward, closing whatever space is left between us, bringing her face closer. "I found pleasure in other ways."

"Like…" She tilts her head, raising an eyebrow.

I take a deep breath, counting to five before releasing it along with the apprehension I have about telling her all about myself and my life. "My father stepped in, educating me about pleasure and control through BDSM."

She blinks again, her lips parted, her breathing a little faster. "Come again?"

"I didn't want a relationship. I wanted casualness and control to feed my appetite and the need I had deep inside me that I never knew existed. My father and mother have another side to them, one many people don't know about outside of the family."

"Your aunt called your mom a sub," Rebel whispers and smiles. "I thought she was talking about a sandwich."

I have to bite my lip to stop myself from laughing at her adorable naïveté. "You're too damn cute, Reb."

She blushes, scraping her fingernails against the sensitive skin on the back of my neck. "I'm not completely clueless, baby," she whispers. "I just never thought your mom…"

"I know. I try to block out any thoughts of my parents having sex, but they are who they are. Didn't really know until my dad pulled my ass to the side, talking to me about finding my center and gaining control of the world around me."

Rebel swallows but doesn't say anything. Her eyes hold mine, her body still, her breathing shallow. "How?" she finally whispers.

"I trained at a local club with a Master my father has been friends with for years. It was the best of both worlds for me at the time. I was able to gain control in

one form and also have consensual physical relationships built on trust, understanding, and sex, but without
the real-world complications I needed to avoid."

"And by complications, I assume you mean relationships and feelings?" she asks.

"I've had relationships with the women at the club,
but they stayed within the walls of the club and never
extended outside. I didn't take them to dinner, bring
them to my house, or even introduce them to anyone in
my family. They were purely about need, want, and
desire. Purely physical and nothing else."

"Why are you telling me this?" she asks, breasts
pressed against me, the heat of her body seeping
through my clothes.

"I want total transparency. You need to know who I
am and how I've changed."

"Baby," she whispers so sweetly my heart beats a
little faster. "I didn't think you were an altar boy. I
figured you worked your way through this little town
before you hit the age of twenty-five."

I shake my head and smile. "You're thinking of the
Rocco you knew. The manwhore I was. But that day…
opened my eyes but crushed my soul."

"I changed too. At first, I partied too hard. Got
involved in some really bad shit and went down a very
dark path. But Adaline changed that, and her biological
father, being the man he was, married me and swore to
provide for us. But after he died, I felt like the world
was against me again until Beau walked into my life."
She sighs and leans forward, resting her forehead

against mine, our bodies connecting almost everywhere. "But I think I was still blinded by my grief and didn't see the man he truly was until it was almost too late. All I've ever wanted was a family and happiness. I never want Adaline to know the sadness I felt as a child. I want her to be happy."

"She is happy, Rebel. The kid is resilient, and her laughter is infectious."

"I see the way she is with you, Rocco. She craves a father figure in her life, and so far, I've failed to deliver."

"You know, the day I left you in the hospital, I told my mother I'd never fall in love and never get involved in a relationship. And until now…I meant every word. I don't know if you could like the new me, but—"

"Could you like the new me?" she shoots back before I have a chance to finish my sentence.

"You're the same you, sweetheart."

She shakes her head as she backs away. "I'm not. I'm a mother with a sordid past and maybe a crazy ex-boyfriend who's searching for me, looking to take me back."

I lift my hand, brushing a few locks of her hair behind her ear, and she moves into my touch. "You're still the same beautiful, wild creature I met ten years ago. Our cores are the same, but our layers have changed, making us into something different. No one has ever made me feel the way you do."

"Rocco," she whispers, stroking my neck with a single finger. "I want this." She pauses, and I tighten my grip on her hip. "I want us. I want whatever this is that burns between us even after all these years."

I lean forward, pressing my mouth to hers, kissing her softly and deeply. She moans, taking what I give without hesitation.

As soon as our mouths part, our eyes are connected, and I need to know if this could happen. "I don't know if I could turn off that other part of me anymore, Rebel. I'm not sure I can give up control all the time, and I'm not sure you could deal with my brand of..."

"Assholiness," she adds, smiling.

"Yeah, sugar. That's one word for it."

"I need you to promise me something before I say yes."

"Anything," I tell her.

"Promise me you won't hurt me and you'll always protect Adaline. No matter what happens, you'll always have her back."

"And yours, Reb. I'll always have your back. If you're going to be mine, I'd take a bullet for you before I'd let anything happen to you. I'd give my life if it meant you were happy."

She slides her hands to cover my mouth. "I've lost too many people, Rocco. Don't jump in front of any bullets and get yourself killed. I don't think I could take another loss."

I kiss her hand before pulling it away. "I'm not going anywhere, sugar. I plan to live a very, very long life."

"Promise me," she begs, moving her hands to my

chest, covering my heart with her palms. "Promise me you won't do anything stupid."

"I won't do anything stupid, but I'll do whatever I have to do to protect what's mine. And that includes you and that little girl sleeping in the next room, dreaming of being a princess."

Rebel's face softens, and she leans into me. "I could easily fall in love with you, Rocco Caldo, and if I'm being honest, I'm scared."

"Me too, sugar. Me too." I lean forward and press my mouth to her soft lips. "Mine," I whisper against her skin.

"Yours," she whispers back.

My hands find her ass, pulling her tight against me before I stand. Her legs lock around my waist, our bodies pressed together at every possible location as I stalk toward the bedroom with Rebel in my arms.

16

REBEL

IT'S BEEN ALMOST A WEEK SINCE I MET HIS FAMILY AND we had "the talk."

Everything has been going great...better than I expected, even, but he hasn't shown his other side, the one he admitted to and warned me about.

Rocco's phone lights up, and I can't help but glance at the screen.

Jade: Tonight at 7 still work?

I turn back toward the window, sipping my coffee, trying not to think too much about Jade.

But I fail.

I have a million questions, and all of them lead to one conclusion. She has to be his girl, or at least, she was until I rolled into town, somehow stealing him away.

She's no one. Stop, Rebel.

"Hey, sugar," Rocco says, moving my hair to the side to press his lips against my neck. "Sleep well?"

I lean into his kiss, loving the way he showers me with affection every moment of the day. "Like a baby."

"Maybe think about moving in to my room," he whispers. "I hate that you leave and crawl back into bed with Adaline. I'd love nothing more than rolling over and being able to sink my cock into you whenever I feel the need."

"And what about my needs?"

He smirks, staring down at me. "Whatever you want, whenever you want it."

My belly flips at the way his dark eyes flicker when he says those words. "I'll remember that."

He moves his mouth closer to my ear, dropping his voice even lower. "My dick is yours, baby. My mouth too. You can wake me up with a face full of pussy, and I'd let you suffocate me in the process."

I smack Rocco's arm, feeling that familiar tingle he still gives me when I think about all the orgasms he's provided me in the past week and how somehow it still feels like it hasn't been enough. "Stop it. Adaline's in the room."

He grabs his phone and moves across the kitchen to the coffeepot, and I can't help but watch him. He turns his screen on, swipes his finger across, and starts to type.

"Everything okay?" I ask, being nosy and unable to stop myself.

"Everything's fine," he tells me.

"Are you working late tonight?" I ask, still wondering about Jade. Even though everything's fine, it doesn't mean he's not texting her back, keeping the date.

Jealousy isn't a good look.

He peers up, making eye contact with me for a brief second. "I don't know yet."

"I need to get a new phone and figure out a car, or maybe we can go get mine up at the cabin."

His fingers stop, and I get his eyes again. "Fuck," he hisses.

"Bad word!" Adaline yells from the living room where she's knee-deep in Barbie bullshit Izzy bought for her.

"I'll leave my SUV here so you can get a phone. And maybe this weekend, we'll go get the car, but I have to talk to Mello and my dad about it first."

I blink, staring at the top of his head when he goes back to typing. "Why do you need to talk to them first?"

"I have my dad tracking Beau," he says like it's not a big deal, which it is, and something he hasn't told me before.

"Since when?"

"Since the beginning."

"You didn't tell me."

He sets his phone down, reaching for a coffee cup and the pot at the same time. "Didn't think I needed to."

I shift in my seat, turning around to face him fully, and pissed doesn't even begin to describe how I feel. "Come again?"

"Sugar," he says, sounding all slick and smooth,

leaving his phone on the counter as he walks across the kitchen, sliding into the seat next to me.

"Don't 'sugar' me, buddy." I poke him in the shoulder, causing his coffee to almost spill over the sides of the mug. "When it comes to Beau, I deserve to know everything."

He sets down the cup and leans on the table, putting his one leg between mine so we're virtually locked together. "I meant to tell you."

"Back it up." I poke him again. "You just said you didn't think you needed to tell me. Which one is it?" I cock my head and narrow my eyes. "Think carefully."

Rocco places his hand on my arm, always maintaining contact with me like it puts me under some weird voodoo spell, which it kind of does, but I'll deny it forever. "I misspoke. I'm sorry. I should've told you, but I didn't want to say anything until I knew more."

I raise an eyebrow and slide toward the edge of my chair until my knee is touching his crotch. "And?"

He swallows, feeling the pressure I'm applying and knowing with one simple move, I could have him in a world of hurt. "Dad said he'd have a full report today. Found out Beau had a mighty long rap sheet. Did you know?"

I jerk my head back, and I blink. "What?"

"Yep, sugar. He isn't a good man. Hell, he was never a good man. Lots of different charges, including domestic violence."

I lean back, letting the back of the chair support me.

"What the fuck," I whisper, realizing I knew nothing about the man I'd been with.

"Even a count of stalking."

"Shit," I mutter. "That's not good."

His other hand lands on my leg, holding my knee with his long, thick fingers. "It's not good. With his history, I'm sure he's looking for you."

My belly drops and suddenly knots as I bow my head, cursing myself for being so stupid. "I'm an idiot."

Rocco lifts his hand, touching my chin, forcing my head upward. "You're not an idiot, Rebel. You're trusting and hopeful."

"Well—" I swallow, pissed off at myself and left with a bitter taste from my mistake "—at least I know you won't be the same problem since you wouldn't even pick up my call and I hadn't heard from you in ten years."

His eyes narrow and he tightens his fingers on my chin, but he doesn't let go. "That's a low blow, sugar, even for you. I'll let it slide, but the next time you give me some shit…"

I hold his gaze, breathing heavy, angry with myself but taking it out on him. "You'll what?" I ask, my voice filled with defiance.

He leans forward, holding my face so I can't back away. His breath moves across my skin, his dark-brown eyes flashing with so much emotion, my palms begin to sweat. "I'll tie you to the bed and make you come so many times, you'll beg me to stop. Beg," he says, drawing out the word until goose bumps spread across my flesh.

I blink as my lips part, trying to imagine a time when I'd ever tell him I didn't want more. Even now, I'd hop on his dick and ride him until I have no more pissed-off in me. "That sounds like torture," I tease, but holy fuck. Holy fuck.

He smirks. "There is such a thing as too much pleasure."

I roll my eyes. "Oh, okay. Whatever you say, big guy."

His smirk grows. "Want to test it out?"

I hold his heated gaze, suddenly forgetting why I was so pissed off in the first place. "Well...I..." I gulp, losing my words.

He stands, towering over me, pinning my back to the chair and getting right in my face. "Tonight, Mama. You better be ready because I'm going to break you in the most delicious way possible."

"Adaline," I whisper. "We can't."

He presses his lips to mine, stealing my breath and my sanity. "Ma will watch her. It's date night." My mouth opens and closes, but nothing comes out. "Hey, Addy," he calls out, turning his face toward her with a devilish smile.

"Yeah, Rocky?" she says, holding a Barbie in each hand.

"Want to spend the night at Izzy's house?"

Her eyes widen, and she gasps before jumping up from the floor, filled with excitement. "Mommy, can I? Please. Please. Please. Please say yes," she begs.

"You play dirty," I whisper in Rocco's ear.

He gives me his eyes again, smile still on his lips. "You haven't seen anything yet, sugar."

I'm stunned speechless. The look in his eyes tells me he's not playing games.

"Mommy, can I?" Adaline asks again when I don't answer.

"Yeah, baby," I whisper, not looking at her but keeping my gaze firmly planted on the predator in front of me. "You can go to Izzy's."

I hear Adaline exclaim, "Yes!" but I'm too busy staring down the man who's threatening me with orgasms, and my body's wiring is going haywire at the veiled threat of pleasure.

"I gotta go, sugar. I'll have Ma pick up Addy at six, and I'll be home shortly afterward. We'll grab her at Grandma's tomorrow."

"Okay," I whisper.

"Good girl," he says back, leaning in and kissing me, taking my words with him as he stalks into the kitchen, sets his mug in the sink, grabs his phone, and strides out the door.

"What did I just do?" I whisper to myself, holding on to the table with one hand, trying to catch my breath.

"I gotta go pack," Adaline says.

"It's only nine, baby."

"I want to be ready," she tells me, sounding way older than she is. "I'm so excited. Which Barbie should

I bring?" She's still holding one in each hand, pushing them in my face.

"Bring all of them. A girl can't have too many."

She turns around, dolls in hand, and skips down the hallway.

Then it hits me, or, I should say, *she* hits me.

Jade.

He didn't mention her or fess up, but whoever she is, he isn't meeting her tonight. At seven, he's going to be giving me his brand of torture, and I am going to be there for every freaking fuckable second.

Nine hours later, I have a new cell phone, a little girl who can't sit still, and so much excitement coursing through my system I think I am liable to have a stroke.

"You look like you're about to jump out of your own skin, dear," Rocco's mom says before she even steps inside.

"Just nervous for a night alone."

She gives me the same shit-eating smirk Rocco's so good at. "I remember what it was like when my mother would take the kids for the night. Just enjoy yourself."

"Izzy!" Adaline runs toward the door, almost knocking me over to get to her.

Izzy's on the ground, one knee resting on the cement, arms open and waiting for Adaline. "Are you ready for tonight, sweet pea?"

"Yes!" Adaline says, wrapping her arms tightly around Izzy's neck. "What are we doing?"

"All the girl things you can imagine. We're going to do mani-pedis and then makeup and hair."

"Pani medis?" Adaline's face scrunches.

"Mani-pedis." Izzy laughs softly and pulls Adaline's arm from around her body. "Mani is for your fingernails. We're going to paint them."

"Can I do yours?"

"Of course." Izzy smiles, and I wonder if she knows what she's in for because the kid can't paint a nail to save her life.

"The best night ever."

"And pedi is for your toes. I bought every shade of pink I could find for your cute little pigs."

Adaline wiggles her pudgy little toes. "A different color for every nail."

"Whatever you want," Izzy tells her before standing and coming face-to-face with me again. "She'll be in safe hands."

"I have no doubt," I tell her honestly. "She's just never stayed at anyone's house. This is the first night she'll ever be away from me."

Izzy touches my arm. "We're only a phone call away, and if she wants to come home, I'll bring her back right away."

I breathe a sigh of relief. "Thank you, Izzy."

"I'll call first, of course. We wouldn't want to interrupt your night alone."

I bite my lip, feeling awkward. "I appreciate that, but if she wants to come home, we can come get her. You're already doing so much to help."

"Just enjoy the silence," she tells me, still touching my arm. "You almost ready, Adaline? Go get your stuff and go potty before we leave. We're going to the store first to grab a few things before we bake cupcakes tonight."

Adaline's mouth drops open, and she's so happy, she only lets out a squeak. A second later, she's gone, and only Izzy and I are left in the room.

"I know you know about Rocco and his tastes," she says, squeezing my arm. "Don't be scared. I was in your shoes a long time ago, but I let go. And let me tell you, girl…best decision of my life."

"I'm super nervous."

She gives me a gentle smile. "Do you have feelings for my son?"

I nod. "If I'm being honest, I always have, and they never went away."

"Just be gentle with him. I know he seems tough, but he's just like his father. They're fiercely protective, love deeply, and they would rather hurt themselves before they ever hurt you. He's gone through a lot, just like you have, Rebel, but he needs you in his life."

"This is crazy," I whisper.

"There's no way to stop fate. When you're meant to be with someone, the world has a way of pushing you back together again. Just open your arms and enjoy the ride, sweetie."

"I'm ready," Adaline says from my side. She's carrying a pink backpack that can't even be zipped up. It looks like she's packed for a longer trip than just an overnight.

"Let's go, beautiful. We have cupcakes to bake and

nails to paint. If we beg, James might let us do his nails too."

"Oh boy," I whisper, finding that hard to imagine.

"He's a sucker for kids. The best dad I've ever seen besides my own, and I'm sure my boys will be the same."

Rocco has been great to Adaline, taking to her like she is his own. I haven't put her to bed a single night since we got here, but that's been her choice and not mine. I had always been her number one, but I knew the kid craved the attention of a man, and she's made it very clear where her heart is going…just like her mother.

I bend down, lifting Adaline's backpack higher up on her shoulder. "Be good for Izzy and James, okay?"

Adaline nods before throwing her arms around me. "I love you, Mommy. I'll be a good girl."

"Love you too, baby." I hug her tightly, fighting back the tears of the first time being away from her.

"Come on, kid. Mommy has to get ready for Rocco to come home. She's going to have a busy night."

I suck in a breath, feeling winded and anxious.

"Relax, Rebel. He'll never hurt you," she tells me. "Never."

"Thanks, Izzy."

She nods. "Just remember to let go and trust that he'll always do right by you."

"I don't trust easy anymore. Too much baggage."

She leans in and hugs me, whispering in my ear, "I know my son, and if there's one person you can trust, it's him."

I give her a quick nod before she takes Adaline's hand and walks out the front door. I stand in the doorway, leaning against the frame, unable to take my eyes off them.

Adaline looks back a few times, waving at me with the biggest smile on her face. My girl is happy. She is happy to be with someone else, and somehow that doesn't hurt my heart. She's found a woman who wants to do all the girl things and who will shower her with attention.

There isn't anything not to love about Rocco's family. Besides him being a dick sometimes, I can't find much wrong with him either.

But the night is young, and I still don't know how I feel about *so many orgasms I'd beg for him to stop.*

17

ROCCO

REBEL'S ON THE COUCH WHEN I WALK IN, FIDGETING with the sleeve of her sweater and looking pale. "Hey," she says as soon as she sees me.

"Hey, sugar. My mom pick up Addy?"

"Yeah. We're alone now."

I can hear the nervousness in her voice.

"You ready to go?" I ask.

"Go?" Her eyes widen, and her leg starts to shake. "Go where?"

"Dinner. I'm starving."

She stares at me, blinking like she doesn't quite understand what I'm saying. "Dinner?"

"Food. I'm taking my girl on a real date."

"But…" She pauses, her gaze moving toward the bedroom. "I thought you said something about all the orgasms."

"That's dessert." I smirk, dipping my head toward

the door. "But first, I'm taking you out for a real meal and a few drinks."

She stands, smoothing out her jeans. "I could eat."

"We haven't had time to talk over a good meal without the kid around. I want to take you out somewhere nice."

She peers down at her outfit. "I'm not really dressed for somewhere nice."

"You look beautiful, Rebel, and it's not that swanky of a joint. Come on, baby. I'm sure you haven't eaten much all day, sitting here wondering about the pleasure I am going to deliver."

She walks toward me, wrapping her arms around my middle as soon as she's close enough. "I thought a lot today," she says, tipping her head back to give me her stunning blue eyes. "About my life, our past, and us."

I put my hands on her ass, staring down at her. "And what did you decide?"

"I thought about slowing things down."

I tighten my fingers around the swell of her ass. "Oh."

Fuck. I was afraid of that. Too much time alone to think isn't always a good thing. She's been through a lot in her life. More than I'll ever know or fully understand. But I'm not them. I'm not her husband from a loveless marriage who got himself killed or a man who'd ever lay his hands on her for any reason.

"Whatever you want, sugar," is all I can say because I'm playing by her rules and timeline. "If you want to slow shit down, we'll slow shit down."

Her eyes soften as my stomach tightens. "Don't you think we're moving too fast?" she asks, placing her hands on my chest.

I take one hand, gripping her wrist, feeling the strong beat of her pulse, remembering the day of the accident and how happy I was to know she was alive. "I don't know about too fast, Reb. I've known you for ten years. Ten years is a long fucking time."

"We haven't seen each other in ten years."

Our bottom halves are pressed together, no space between, both of our hearts racing. "Doesn't mean I didn't think about you every day. Figured I'd never see you again, but I still didn't stop seeing you in my dreams every night."

She bends her neck, resting it on my pec beside her hand. "But what if this doesn't work out?"

Kissing the top of her head, I mumble, "Then at least we know we tried. I'm not willing to just let you go without at least seeing what this could be. But if you want to walk away, please wait until I know you're going to be safe, and Addy too."

"I love that you call her that," she whispers into my shirt, curling her fingers around the material. "I've never felt as safe as I do in your arms, Rocco. Never knew the peace I feel when I'm with you. I don't know how to process or accept the happiness."

I raise my hand to her chin and tip her head back using my fingertips. "You deserve happiness, and I want to be the one to give it to you, sugar. Let's go to dinner, hang out, have a proper date, and we'll slow things down. Once the storm passes, if you want to go, I won't stop you. It'll hurt, baby, but I can deal with my own pain better than I can deal with others'."

She stares up at me with water rimming her eyes. "How did I get so lucky?"

"I'm the lucky one," I say. "Didn't think I'd ever find this feeling again, but you're here and I'm feeling everything deep. So damn deep, I'll go at your speed as long as you feel safe, baby."

She lifts up on her toes, pressing her lips to mine, kissing me so gently my heart flutters. "Dinner would be perfect."

I smile down at her, holding her face in my hand. "Whatever you want."

"Rocco," she whispers, staring at me with her blue eyes. "We can still have sex, though, right?"

I can't stop myself from turning my face toward the ceiling and bursting into laughter. "God, you're so fucking cute, Rebel. My cock is yours. Whatever you want, whenever you want it."

"I like that," she tells me as she wipes her eyes, the tears subsiding as quickly as they came. "I like that a lot."

A half hour later, we slide into a booth at Salvatore's, the best damn Italian food in the county besides my grandmother's. It's tucked away, hidden, and a treasure only the locals know about.

"Rocco," the owner, a man named Martin, greets as we walk through the door. His arms instantly open, welcoming us.

My hand is at the small of Rebel's back, moving her with me into the small entryway near the hostess stand. "You're looking well," I tell him, exchanging the customary half-ass kiss on each cheek.

"So do you, my boy," he says before his eyes drift to Rebel and brighten. "Who do we have here?"

"Martin, this is Rebel, my..."

What do I call her? I want to say she's my girlfriend, but she wants to take it slow. Friend sounds too casual, and I rarely, if ever, touch my friends in the way I'm touching her.

"His girlfriend," Rebel says at my side, finishing the sentence for me to end the awkward pause I created.

"*Bella*," Martin whispers before taking Rebel's hand in his and kissing the top. "Rocco has the finest taste in food and women."

Rebel blushes but doesn't pull her hand away when Martin lingers a little longer than I like. "Thank you," she says softly.

I clear my throat, staring at Martin a little bit more harshly when he doesn't let her go. "You done?"

Martin glances up, winking at me. "It's not often we have such beautiful creatures in here."

I roll my eyes. "Martin, you're a shit liar."

"New ones, then." He smiles and touches his chest after he finally releases her hand. "Let an old man enjoy himself for a minute. One day, you'll be old too, and you'll realize you have very few charms left."

I shake my head, trying to hold back my laughter. "I

know what your wife looks like, Martin, and she's stunning."

"Jade," he calls out over his shoulder, and Rebel's body stiffens. "Rocco's here."

A dark-haired beauty with the most captivating green eyes glides out from the dining room. "Ah, Rocco. I'm so happy you were able to make it." Jade's eyes flicker to Rebel with a small smile. "We are beyond delighted to have you here tonight." Jade presses her body against Martin's, touching his chest. "Martin had the chef prepare a special menu for you and your special guest."

I dip my chin, giving Jade a smile. "Jade, I'd like you to meet my girlfriend, Rebel."

Jade smiles at Rebel, appraising her. "It's lovely to meet you. Rocco is one of our favorite customers, but he's usually alone or with his brother. This is a special occasion, and we're going to make your night perfect. I hope you enjoy the food."

"Thank you, Jade," Rebel says, returning the smile, but it barely reaches her eyes.

I'm not sure what the fake smile is about, but the tension coming off Rebel is palpable.

"I appreciate you making tonight happen. I know you're usually closed tonight, Jade. It means a lot."

"You're like family, kid," she tells me, which earns her a laugh. "Let me show you to your table."

"I'll grab a bottle of our best wine," Martin tells us, holding up a finger. "Only the best for you two lovebirds."

"I don't remember the last time I saw that man in such a romantic mood," Jade says, motioning for us to follow.

Once at the table, I pull out Rebel's chair, waiting for her to sit before tucking her underneath.

This night isn't going to go exactly as I planned. I didn't think she was going to tell me we needed to slow things down, but I completely understand. Hopefully I can use my charm and sexual persuasion to get her to change her heart and mind.

"It's beautiful here," Rebel says, glancing around the restaurant, soaking in the ambiance.

"It's very exclusive and very few people know about it, but I wanted to treat you to something special tonight."

She looks so beautiful in the soft glow of the lighting above us and the single candle on the table.

"So, Jade..." Rebel whispers, leaning forward when she says her name. "You know her well?"

I tilt my head, staring at Rebel, wondering what she's getting at. "Jade's been a friend for many years."

"Have you slept with her?"

"She's Martin's wife, Rebel."

"Not an answer."

This is a tricky situation. Technically, I have slept with Jade, but it was years ago, before she met Martin and was swept away by his good looks and his amazing cooking skills. Jade and I played at a club in downtown Tampa for a month. She always wanted more, but I wasn't able to give it. Once Martin laid eyes on her, our casual relationship ended.

"Have you slept with her?" Rebel asks again.

"A long time ago, Rebel. A long, long time ago," I admit, shifting my weight forward, hating to tell her this. But in the name of truth and transparency, I can't hide what had happened between us, no matter how short or insignificant.

Rebel's gaze moves to where Jade's standing across the way, grabbing two wineglasses. "Does her husband know?" Rebel whispers.

"I introduced them," I tell her, which gets me two raised eyebrows.

"Really?"

I nod. "Martin's a great guy, and Jade wanted stability and more than I could offer. I knew they'd be the perfect fit."

Rebel leans closer, her elbows on the table, her face aglow in the candlelight. "He doesn't feel weird about you being near his wife?"

I shake my head. "They're married, sugar. He knows as well as I do the importance of the promise and commitment they made to each other. It's a line I'd never cross even if she begged, which she hasn't. I moved on, and clearly, so did she."

"So, like…" Rebel looks around, seeing where Jade is before she says, "That's it? They don't come to the club anymore? They just left?"

I clasp my hands around hers, not answering when I see Jade come our way. This is going to be a long conversation, and I can see in Rebel's eyes this isn't the end of the questions.

"Here we go," Jade says softly as she places two glasses on the table. "Martin should be here with the wine any minute. I'll have the chef prepare your appetizer first. I hope you're hungry because you two are in for an absolute treat."

"Thank you, Jade," I tell her, giving her a smile, remembering the sweet person she was and not the sexual being.

Jade gazes at Rebel and smiles, not getting one in return this time before scurrying away into the kitchen.

"Be nice, Rebel. Jade's done nothing wrong."

"I am nice."

I smirk, studying her face and the way her lips are pinched. "Are you jealous?"

"No."

That's a hard yes. I like seeing the jealousy in her eyes, especially after she said she wanted to take things slow. Maybe it wasn't the kiss of death, but instead a way for her to guard her heart.

"You are."

She leans back, dropping her arms into her lap. "It's just really strange."

"Here we are," Martin says, holding a bottle of red wine in one hand and showing it to me. "Good?"

"Perfect, Martin." I give him a smile, dipping my chin when his eyes meet mine.

Under any other circumstances, seeing Martin and Jade would be normal, but with Rebel and how quickly she caught on to our history, it's more than awkward. Things like this are bound to happen living in a town so small and with the way I blew through women over the last ten years.

Martin makes quick work of pouring our wine before leaving us alone again, joining his wife in the kitchen.

We have the dining room to ourselves again, and I use the time to try to be as informative and open as possible. "Have you ever run into someone you've slept with before while out in public?"

"Well, yeah. Of course."

"Was it weird?"

"No."

"Did you feel something for them even after a long time of not being with them?"

"Of course not."

"It's the same, Rebel. Martin and Jade are my friends. Our community at the club is small, and we're friends above everything else. We respect one another's boundaries, and when sexual relationships are severed, there's still respect and friendship afterward. I love Martin and Jade like family, but nothing more than that. They feel the same. How did you even know about it to ask?"

She lets out a long, dramatic exhale. "I saw her text this morning."

It all clicks. Rebel and I were fine, and then I walked out of the bedroom and she changed. Something had changed her, and it was nothing I did. She went from running super-hot to luke-fucking-warm in a matter of hours.

"I thought you were meeting a woman named Jade tonight for sex. I'm sorry I looked—"

I lift my hand. "It's fine, sugar. I was just trying to surprise you and didn't even think about Jade texting me. I'll be sure to be more mindful in the future."

"No. Don't," she tells me, giving me her eyes, the softness back in her face. "I shouldn't be so sensitive. I'm still learning the new you, and with me just showing up, I'm sure I've cut off someone's time with you."

"I haven't been to the club in almost a year. You haven't taken me from anyone, and even if there had been anyone, I would've quickly ended things with them the moment you walked back into my life."

She leans her body back over the table, putting one hand on her wineglass and the other one near her napkin. "So, there's no one else?"

I reach across, covering her hand with mine again. "No one else, Rebel. Only you."

She smiles a genuine smile. "The only one," she repeats.

"It's always been you."

In this moment, I know I need to do everything possible to make Rebel understand there has never been nor will ever be anyone else except her.

18

REBEL

My lips are on Rocco's before the front door closes. He snakes his arms around my back, and I use the opportunity to wrap my arms around his neck and my legs around his middle.

He kisses me back, hard and deep, making my toes curl in my sandals.

I want this.

The date nights.

The candlelight.

The honesty.

When he looks at me, I feel like the most special girl in the world. I don't feel like a run-down mom with stretch marks and bags under my eyes from the stress that's etched on my face after decades of bullshit.

Rocco makes me feel beautiful.

He does that.

No one else did.

Not Collin. Not Beau.

I didn't feel cherished in the same way, but I allowed myself to be used, searching for the happiness I thought I'd find in their arms. But I knew where it was all along.

I'd only felt it once before, and it was ten years ago, before we were torn apart by a tragedy that had scarred us both.

"I want you," I whisper against his lips.

He tightens his arms, pressing my body flat against his. He is hard everywhere I am soft and big where I am little.

I love feeling small in his arms and the way his body envelops me when he holds me, kissing me rough and hard like he is now.

He moves through the living room with me in his arms, holding on tight, unwilling to let me go. When his ass hits the couch, his cock presses into my pussy, sending a jolt of pleasure through me.

My fingers move to the bottom of his T-shirt, yanking it upward, breaking the kiss to lift it over his head and exposing his rock-hard body.

"Your body's fucking amazing," I whisper in the faint glow from the streetlights streaming through the bank of windows in the living room.

His hands are on my ass, kneading each cheek as I gawk at him. "Sugar, you're the one who's amazing." He runs his finger over my cleavage, setting my skin on fire with the soft touch. "Every inch of your body is a playground built for my pleasure."

My core convulses and he smirks. Wait. *Did he…* I cock my head.

"I felt it."

"Felt what?" I ask, stilling in his lap.

"The way your pussy twitched."

My eyebrows rise. "What?" I whisper.

"I can always feel how much you need and want me when you're in my lap, pressed against my dick, with only a small scrap separating our bodies."

Fuck. Talk about embarrassing and something I never realized. I'm pretty sure most women don't either.

"Now give me your mouth again."

Without hesitation, I lean forward, touching my mouth to his, loving the way his lips still taste of wine but sweeter.

My hands roam his upper body, gliding over the silky smoothness of his skin. His body has changed so much from when we were practically kids, but definitely for the better.

One of his hands leaves my back, moving to my neck, gripping me from behind. I gasp into his mouth, loving the roughness of his touch.

"You like that, Rebel?" he murmurs, not giving me a chance to answer with words because my body does it for him. He grunts, feeling the twitch, which I seem to be powerless to stop.

My body is a traitor, and my pussy is a whore. Definitely a whore when it comes to Rocco Caldo.

He tightens his fingers around the sides of my neck, holding my head in place, controlling the depth of his kiss. I can feel his hunger as his tongue slips between my lips, dancing with mine.

I flatten my palms, letting him take me where he wants, giving in to him and his touch completely. Straddling his legs, I'm his to take and powerless to stop him. I've always been a sucker for him, and time hasn't changed the way my body craves his touch.

My fingers drift lower, following the line between his abs until they land on his jeans. He doesn't stop me as I undo the button, pulling the zipper down slowly. He raises his hips, and I yank down the denim, freeing his hard length. My fingers are around the thickness a second later, stroking him firmly and long, paying careful attention to the tip.

He moans into my mouth as his fingers tighten around my neck a little more, totally restricting my ability to move my head. Electric shocks scatter across my body as I move my hand faster, stroking him with the speed at which I wish he were fucking me.

When his hand leaves my neck, I feel naked, but his lips never go away. I shiver as his fingertips slide under my T-shirt, lifting the material over my stomach. I raise my hands, moving my lips away from his for only a second for him to pull it over my head.

My bra is nothing for a man as experienced as him. One hand and it's gone, discarded to the floor like it is meaningless.

He pats my ass, saying, "Up, baby. Take them off."

I moan in agitation, not wanting to get off him or

remove my hands from the dick I've been enjoying stroking for a few minutes.

But when I stand, with the way he looks at me and the heat in his eyes, I still feel connected with him.

"Go slow," he tells me when I hook my fingers into the waistband of my pants.

I push them down, about to bend forward, when he moves his hand to his cock, wraps his fingers around where mine have just been, and starts to work it in the same way I did.

My lips part as I watch him touch himself, wondering how many times he's done that and thought of me.

I bend over, slowly pushing my pants down my legs but getting my face closer to his impressive package. He does stroke the same way, twisting his hand slightly when he reaches the top, yanking on it harder than I could've possibly imagined would be pleasurable.

His eyes roam over my body, moving from my breasts to my stomach and down to the hair between my legs when I stand. My younger self waxed often, but the mom in me doesn't find it practical anymore.

"You're perfect, Rebel," he whispers, his voice deep and thick.

I feel beautiful when he says those words and with the way his eyes rake over me, full of hunger. I drop my panties on top of the pile with my other clothes, standing before him completely naked.

"Crawl to me," he says. "Wrap those pretty red lips around my cock."

I don't even think as I bend my knees, finding the hardwood floor, and I move my body in his direction in the most catlike way I've ever moved in my life.

Placing my hands on his jeans, I lift myself up as he pushes his cock down toward my lips. I open my mouth, stick out my tongue, waiting for him to give me a taste of the piece of him I've wanted inside me since the last time.

He doesn't force it down my throat, but instead slides it slowly across my tongue, hitting every taste bud with his hard softness. I stare up at him, his eyes pinned on mine as he lifts his hips, guiding his dick into my mouth.

I close my lips, sucking on him as he pulls out even slower before sliding it back inside.

"Do it slow, baby. I want to enjoy this," he says, releasing his hand from around his cock, giving me control.

I put my hands where his have been, working his length while paying special attention to the tip with my mouth.

His fingers tangle in my hair, guiding me up and down, but not being forceful, which is a nice change. I love the way he tastes, the soft moans leaving his lips, and how his hips move with me and chase my mouth.

I smile around his dick, humming my appreciation as he shivers. I feel powerful like this, with my hands around him, sucking him off.

But far too quickly, his hands are under my arms, lifting me in the air and planting me in his lap. "Ride me, baby. Fuck me how you want to be fucked," he rasps.

And I do. His hands are on my hips the entire time, tethering him to me as I ride his cock like I am a cowgirl. It feels like I do this forever, but it is probably only a few minutes before my knees start to shake and my motion begins to slow. That's when Rocco's hands go to my waist, lifting me up before slamming me down on his cock, keeping the same rhythm I'd set but haven't been able to maintain.

I lean forward, taking his mouth as he uses my body to fuck us both. My hands on his shoulders help keep me from falling over as I bounce on his body, powerless to stop him. My toes curl and my muscles tighten as his length strokes me from the inside, driving me closer to an orgasm I know will do me in.

Only one.

Not two.

Not three.

I only need to have one orgasm delivered by him to render me unable to speak or move. And when that orgasm comes, that's exactly what happens.

He follows me over the edge, grunting through each thrust until his hands still. "Fuck," he hisses, loosening his pinching grip on my hips, both of us panting and sweaty.

"We sure did," I whisper before falling face first into his chest, unable to even sit up.

"I could do this every night, sugar."

I like the sound of that, and so does my pussy—even

though I just came, because it spasms, which is immediately met with his chuckle.

"Again?" I murmur against the soft skin between his pecs.

"Again."

I squeeze my eyes shut, sighing. "Well, now I know."

"I do too, but that isn't news."

"You hear that?" I ask, hearing nothing except for our breaths and the sound of our hearts pounding.

"Peace?" he answers.

"Yeah. It's so quiet."

"I love that kid, baby, but a night alone has been nice. She brings joy to this house. A happiness I haven't felt in here in a long time, but I needed tonight alone with you."

I smile against his skin. "Think we can still take it slow?"

"I'll do whatever you want, Reb, but there's nothing in me that wants to go slow. I've done slow. I've done the alone thing for ten fucking years, and now that you're back...I'm not ready for slow."

I push up, staring into his eyes. "I don't want slow either," I admit. "You make me feel alive. So freaking alive and, for the first time in my life, as if someone actually cares about me."

"My dick did all that, baby?"

I push myself up and smack at his chest playfully. "Your dick is fabulous, sweetie, but it's not a miracle worker."

"Like fuck, it isn't," he teases, smiling at me.

"It is when you aren't being a cocky asshole."

"I'm never a cocky asshole," he argues.

I raise an eyebrow, no smile on my face. "You're eighty percent cocky asshole and twenty percent sweetness."

"Five percent sweetness and fifteen percent pussy whisperer."

I roll my eyes. "There's the eighty coming out in you."

"The fifteen just made you come."

"Whatever. I'm being serious."

"Me too," he tells me, running his hands up and down my back as I straddle his legs, my toes barely touching the floor. "There's nothing about us that doesn't work, Rebel."

I stare at him, hating that he's right. "I know. But I want to take this slow, and I don't know how to do that with you."

"Someday, I'll put a ring on that finger. But until then, we just do what we do. Live life a little. Enjoy each other for a little while. Settle into whatever this is, and when we're ready, we'll take it to the next level."

My gaze drops to my hands when his stare becomes too much, just like his words. "Should I move out? I mean, maybe we need—"

"No," he interrupts me. "Don't do that unless you think it's absolutely necessary."

"Well, I..." I glance back up, finding his eyes

watching me, always studying my expression. "I don't have the money to move anywhere else right now."

"Stay with me, sugar. Later, after you get on your feet, if you want your own place, we'll make it happen."

I swallow and blink, confused as to how well he seems to be taking this and even offering up a way that would work for both of us. "You wouldn't be mad?" I whisper.

He shakes his head, his hands splayed out across my back, his thumbs resting near my ass. "I wouldn't be mad at all. I want your happiness more than I want my own."

Then my mind moves to Adaline. She's been nothing but smiles since we got here, quickly getting attached to Rocco. "Addy needs to get enrolled in school. I know it's only pre-K, but it's—"

"We'll do it Monday."

"You'd go with me?"

"Rebel. If we're going to be a we, we're going to be a we. It's not you and then me—it's us. We're an *us*, babe."

Wow. I love that. Completely different from Beau and Collin, where they did their thing and never got involved in my life unless it was something that pissed them off...which, with Beau, seemed to be daily.

"We're an us."

He taps my butt, giving me a signal. "Up, sweetheart. I could use a shower. You want to join me?"

I climb off, almost collapsing on my shaky legs until

he catches me with one hand. "I think I need to sit here a while."

He smiles, moving my ass to the couch and standing in front of me, jeans still on but his cock out. "Just rest a bit. I'll bring you to bed when I'm done."

I relax into the cushions, loving the softness against my skin, which probably has a zipper impression somewhere between my legs. "You'll bring me to bed?"

"You're exhausted. Lemme spoil you."

"Spoil me?"

"Close your eyes," he says, leaning over and giving me a kiss. "I'll grab you for bed when I'm done."

"Okay," I say with a small smile, holding back a yawn I know is ready to overtake me.

He doesn't make it two feet before his jeans are gone and he's kicking them in the air, catching them in his hand.

It is a nice view is my last thought before I close my eyes, letting the darkness and exhaustion take me.

19

ROCCO

"REBEL," GIGI CALLS, MOTIONING FOR MY GIRL TO GO sit with the other women at the table on the lanai.

"Go ahead, sugar. I'm sure the girls want all the dirt. Just don't listen to their bullshit."

She smiles up at me, giving me a small kiss. "I want all the dirt."

"You're too jealous for all the dirt."

Her lips flatten.

"See. Right there. Too jealous and I like you that way."

Her eyebrows knit together. "You do?"

"I like it better than you not giving a shit."

"I've never been the jealous type."

"I like that even more," I whisper against her lips, staring into her deep-blue eyes.

"Stop sucking face and get your ass over here."

"I like them," she says to me, talking about my cousins after spending an hour with them last weekend.

219

"They like you too."

"It's nice to be around other moms."

"You can have more time with them next week. We're leaving right after dinner to grab your car."

"I can't wait to have my own car again."

"What's wrong with the truck?"

"I practically need a stepladder to get into it. It's not practical."

"Whatever you say, babe."

"Girl, don't make us come over there and drag you away from that man!" Tamara hollers out, pushing her chair back.

"Gotta go," Rebel says, leaving my arms without another kiss.

"You ladies behave."

"Fuck off," Gigi tells me, lifting her middle finger in the air. "Go find the guys and talk guy shit."

"What the hell is guy shit?"

Gigi shrugs. "Don't know. Don't care. This is girl time, and you're not invited."

"I feel slighted," I tease, smiling and returning the sweet gesture.

Tamara, Gigi, Lily, and Jo all stare at me, no smiles on their faces, looking at me like I am the enemy.

I don't know what their men did wrong, but something is happening. I didn't need to be a psychic to know when shit is off, and shit is definitely off.

All four are married with kids of their own and to men who aren't easy to live with. I know because they are cut from the same wood as me, bossy and no bullshit. That causes issues since three of the four are Gallo girls, and they don't put up with their men's attitudes or the shit that comes with them.

"Who the fuck did something wrong?" I ask, collapsing back into the couch in the den where the guys have made a home to watch the football game. Our parents are all sitting in the living room next to the kitchen, and as the family grew, we started to separate sometimes, especially when we wanted to talk away from them.

"Mammoth," Pike, Gigi's husband, says, his eyes never leaving the television. "He fucked up."

"Bullshit," Mammoth mutters, lifting a beer to his lips, his ankle resting on top of the opposite knee, looking chill. "I'm innocent."

Carmello chuckles, holding out a beer to me, one he's been saving because he always has my back. "Tamara walked in on some chick coming on to Mammoth and lost her shit."

"How is that his fault?" I ask.

"She said I didn't do enough to stop the woman from flirting with me." Mammoth shrugs, tipping back his head, taking a swig of his beer. "The woman is off-the-charts hormonal."

"You should tell her that," my cousin Nick teases, knowing how well she'd take that comment.

"I'd like to get pussy again in my lifetime, so I'll pass on that shit-ass advice, asshole. It's my dumb-ass fault for knocking her up again."

My eyebrows rise, and I almost choke on my beer. "Fuckin' again?"

He smirks, resting his beer on his thigh. "Yep. Couldn't keep her off my dick, and we wanted another kid anyway."

I pound on my chest, trying to clear the beer and puke that are clogging my throat. "That's my cousin you're talking about."

"I know, man. Can't help that shit. But, fuck me," he mutters, glancing up at the ceiling, "She gets so fucking territorial when she's pregnant. I can't even be in the vicinity of another woman without her wanting to murder one of us or both."

"Wish you luck with that one, brother." Pike tips his beer toward Mammoth along with his chin. "She's always been a wild one."

"I wouldn't have her any other way. She's my wildcat."

Carmello elbows me, glancing at me out of the corner of his eye. "What's wrong? You seem off."

"Nothing, man." I blow out a breath, relaxing back into the couch. "Just want to kick back and hang with my girl, but gotta take a drive up to the cabin to get her car."

"You want company? I can drive her car back so she doesn't have to follow you."

My brother is solid. A pain in the ass sometimes, but always there for me even when I've tried like hell to push him away.

"That would work. You don't mind?"

"Got nothing else to do. Six hours in the car sounds like a great time," he mutters, and I know he doesn't mean it, but he's doing me a favor because that's what we do.

"We're leaving after dinner."

"Not a problem. I'll be ready," he tells me, tapping his bottle against mine. "I could use a ride to clear my head."

"Bad day?"

"Bad fucking week, brother. Crazy-ass dreams."

"Carrie?" I ask and he grimaces.

"I love you having Rebel back in your life, but it brought up a bunch of shit I thought I had buried so deep it wouldn't find me again."

"You need to talk?"

He shakes his head. "I'll work it out. I always do. Just got to work through it and maybe go back to talk to someone who's impartial to help me sort out whatever it is still festering inside me."

I know what eats at him. He was driving the car when Carrie died. It could've been either of us behind the wheel, and the shit would've ended the same way. He felt the guilt about driving the car, while the image of her dying in my arms ate at my insides for years.

"We'll get through this. We always do. I'm here for you...whatever you need."

"I know you are. Therapy helped you."

"And Dad," I remind him. "The club gave me an escape."

"I haven't been there in years."

"Go back. Lose yourself for a while."

He nods. "I may just do that."

"But I can't come with you this time."

He shrugs. "You got yourself a good woman. You don't need what the club has to offer."

"Can't argue with that," I tell him, moving my arm around the back of the couch, pulling him closer. "I love you, Carm."

"Love you too, Roc. You're the only person who understands how I feel, what I feel, and how deep it runs."

"Dinner," Ma says, poking her head into the study, eyeing all the guys. "If any of you can tear yourself away from the Tampa Bay game long enough to choke down some noodles." She's gone as quickly as she walked in, the door left open.

"They've lived here longer than they lived in Chicago, but they're still loyal to them Bears."

Jett, Lily's husband, shrugs. "Some people like the pain."

"That ain't no lie," I mutter, knowing how deep this family's love for Chicago sports runs, even though they haven't won shit in decades. "Let's eat and get out of here. It's going to be a long day."

"I'm fucking ready for it," Mello says, rising to his feet. "Let's go, fuckers. I don't need my mom coming back and busting our balls."

They move their asses, not wanting the wrath of Izzy Caldo either. Minutes later, our plates are full of food, and we're scattered around the house, stuffing our faces.

"Mello's coming with us," I tell Rebel as she sits next to me, moaning with each bite. "But you're making it pretty fucking hard for me not to think about fucking you first."

"We don't have time for all that," she tells me, moaning again and smiling.

"Baby, I can be fast," I promise her.

She shakes her head. "Not at your grandma's house. Are you insane?"

I shrug. "I tried."

"Eat your food," she tells me. "The quicker we leave, the earlier we'll be home."

I wink at her.

"You sure your mom is okay watching Addy another night?"

I tick my chin in the direction of my mother. "What do you think?"

Addy's in the chair next to her, mimicking my mother in every way, from the way she sits to how she holds her spoon.

"My mother is in heaven after having three sons. Hey, Ma," I call out, and her eyes instantly find me. "Can you watch Adaline until we get back from the cabin later?"

Adaline wiggles in her seat with a giant smile on her face as she stares up at my mother like they're new best friends. "Please," Addy whispers.

"She can stay the night again. You two kids take

your time. We're going to watch movies and eat popcorn." My mom puts her arm around Addy. "What do you want to watch tonight?"

"Princesses."

Mom smiles. "So much better having a girl around the house."

"Whatever," I mutter, looking back at Rebel. "Taken care of, sugar."

"I thought my kid would miss me a little bit," Rebel says, watching her daughter with my mother, "but I'm not even mad."

"Mom will take good care of her, and that means we get another night alone." I waggle my eyebrows. "Orgasms for everyone."

"Shh," Rebel says, peering around the room from under her lashes. "Someone's going to hear you."

"They all have orgasms too, or else there wouldn't be all these people here."

"Oh Jesus," Rebel whispers. "Eat your food so we can go, and stop talking."

I laugh, going back to my pasta and meatballs, ready to get the drive over with so I can be in my girl, giving her all the pleasure she wants without a tiny human in the next room.

Four hours later, we pull down the long dirt road leading to the cabin. The three of us spent the drive enjoying music, singing at the top of our lungs to our favorites, and dancing in our seats to the ones that made our bodies move.

It was a light trip, the same carefree attitude we felt

when we were younger. The same easiness we felt when Carrie was alive and we were heading toward a weekend of fun and frolic.

Carmello's door is open before I cut the engine. "I'll go turn on the outdoor lights. I just gotta grab something from the safe," he says, jumping out from the back and taking off toward the front door.

"I need to go in too," she says, giving me a small smile. "Mom bladder."

I nod, knowing we have another three hours back and not much in between except for forest, and pissing in the woods isn't something most chicks dig. "We have time. We're not in a rush, baby."

"Good," she says as I lift her hand to my mouth, brushing my lips over her skin. "We don't need to leave right away. Let's stretch our legs and grab something to drink from the fridge. There's no rush. The sun's already setting."

"Thank you for this," she says.

"For what?"

"For bringing me back to my car."

"It's your car, Rebel. We weren't just going to abandon it forever, but we couldn't risk you taking it with us when there was so much we didn't know about Beau. I still need to check it for a tracker before we go."

"I don't think he's coming for me."

"He's been missing since you left. He could be anywhere."

She frowns. "I was so stupid."

"Nah, baby. You weren't stupid. You were trusting

and naïve to the extent a person will go to find someone."

"I learned my lesson."

"And yet you're still with me."

She rolls her eyes. "I doubt you'd chase after me."

I smile. "I'd chase you, Rebel, but I would never give you a reason to run. When a man has feelings for a woman, he treats her like a queen and never gives her a reason to leave."

"I know," she whispers. "I've never had anyone put me first. Never in my entire life."

I hate that her life experiences have been total shit. She deserved better as a little girl and even more so as an adult. "You have it now, baby."

She smiles at me, lighting up completely and making my heart swell. "I gotta pee," she says softly, squirming in her seat.

"Well, go get it, mama. I'll be under your car, checking shit out."

She nods, reaching for the door handle before peeling out, following in Carmello's footsteps.

I watch her stalk up the drive, run up the front steps, and disappear inside before I get to work underneath her car.

REBEL

"WE GOT MOTION," CARMELLO SAYS, STARING DOWN AT his phone as we stand inside the kitchen, Rocco still outside.

"We have motion?" I ask, staring at him funny.

"Outside." Carmello's eyes move toward the door. "Rocco isn't alone."

A knot forms in my stomach, and I know without having to be told. We're in the middle of nowhere. People don't just show up unless they're looking, and there's only one man searching for me.

It's Beau, and he's not here for a friendly visit.

He's been waiting for me, knowing where I'd been. No doubt, there was a tracker on my car, or he'd used my old cell phone's location.

If we would've stayed, he would've...

"Don't move," Carmello tells me, pointing to the very spot I'm standing. "I'm grabbing a gun from the safe. Do not go outside under any circumstances."

I slide my eyes to the front door and then back to Carmello as he walks into the bedroom. I know he said to stay here, but Rocco's outside.

I gulp, pushing down the knowledge of how bad things could've been if Carmello and Rocco hadn't convinced me to go with them.

But now...now, Rocco is in Beau's cross hairs.

Beau is here for me, and I have no doubt he'll do whatever he can to make sure my ass is in his car, heading back with him, even if that means hurting Rocco and Carmello.

Without thinking, I head to the door, leaving Carmello in the bedroom, and step out onto the front porch.

I gasp when I see Beau's arm outstretched, a gun in his hand and pointed directly at Rocco.

"Rebel," Beau says as he faces me, Rocco between the two of us, standing still. "I've been looking for you, baby."

Rocco shakes his head as I move forward, walking down the stairs on shaky legs.

"You found me, Beau. Leave Rocco alone."

"Oh, this is the great Rocco you've talked about. I thought the man would be—" Beau shakes the gun at Rocco "—better."

"Please, Beau. He doesn't matter. Let's go, honey, and leave Rocco here. Take me home," I tell him, somehow getting those words out without my voice shaking in fear.

"No," Rocco says, taking a step forward to stop me.

"Stop moving," Beau says before Rocco can get within a few feet of me. "I will shoot you."

My stomach turns at the thought. "You don't want to shoot anyone," I say, knowing he does and it's probably me.

But I'll sacrifice myself for a short time to keep Rocco alive. He'd find me. He'd save me. I know he'd stop at nothing until he got me back and Beau ended up right where he belonged.

"I'll go," I tell him, moving past Rocco, making eye contact and giving him a sorrowful smile. "You don't need to force me or hurt him."

"Get your ass in the truck," Beau tells me, ticking his chin toward his beat-up white pickup.

He doesn't even ask about Adaline, never giving two shits about her. It was always me. Only me he wanted, and he was completely transparent about that. Adaline was an inconvenience in his eyes and nothing more.

"Okay," I whisper, looking over at Rocco as he stiffens.

"Do not move," Rocco tells me, and Beau starts to advance on him.

I dash between them, ready to give myself up and do anything in my power so no one gets hurt, especially not Rocco.

But when Beau reaches out to touch me, Rocco pushes me aside. I fall to the ground, my palms smashing into the gravel.

Rocco moves quickly, punching Beau in the face,

causing his head to snap back. I watch as he doesn't stop, advancing on Beau, hitting him repeatedly until Beau's body hits the ground next to me and the gun skids across the way.

I think Rocco's going to stop, but I'm wrong. He's on top of Beau, holding him by the collar of his shirt, pounding him in the face as blood starts to splatter everywhere, staining the rocks red around him.

"Rocco," I call out. "Stop."

Oh my God.

Rocco's going to kill Beau. I've never seen him so mad. His face doesn't even look like the same man I've started falling in love with.

"Fuck him. The. Bastard. Doesn't. Get. To. Hurt. You." Each word is short and followed by another blow to Beau's body.

"Fuck!" Carmello exclaims, coming out of the cabin too late, but brandishing a shotgun. "Jesus Christ."

He drops the shotgun in the grass before rushing over to Rocco, hauling him off Beau.

I watch in horror, shocked by the amount of blood and how easily Rocco's switch flipped, turning him into someone I've never seen before.

He's always been gentle with me and everyone around him, but he turned into a different man with Beau.

"Stop," Carmello tells him, lifting Rocco's feet off the ground, but his arms continue to swing around. "You've done enough damage."

"Fuck him. He does not get to hurt my girl," Rocco spits, his face red and furious.

I lift myself up and dust off my hands of the tiny rocks that have embedded in my flesh. A searing pain shoots through my hands, the stones having made dozens of tiny cuts.

"Rebel," Rocco says, his voice gentler as Carmello lets him go, and he's immediately at my side.

"Stop," I tell him, raising my bloody palm between us. "Don't."

His brown eyes meet mine, the heat of the moment still coursing through him, although his face is just as gentle as it always is with me. "You're hurt."

"You pushed me, Rocco. This is what happens when you push someone to the ground."

"Sugar, I needed you away from him. I couldn't do shit with you standing between us, and there was no way in hell I was going to let that man touch you again or get off a shot."

That sounds nice. Really nice. And it is sweet, but the way he turned into another human being, almost animalistic, frightened the hell out of me.

"I need a minute," I whisper, gazing from him to my scraped-up palms, my heart hurting more than my flesh.

"He would've killed you," Rocco says, kneeling next to me and trying to take my hands in his, but I quickly pull them back.

"He could've killed you," I remind him, throwing out the simple fact that he very well could have taken a bullet and Beau wouldn't have thought twice about pulling the trigger.

"Sheriff's on the way," Carmello says behind us, neither one of us paying attention to him.

Tears sting my eyes, the pain in my hands and my heart mingling together. "I did this," I tell him. "I brought him here."

"Sugar," Rocco whispers, reaching for my chin, capturing it between his fingers before I have a chance to pull back. "You did nothing. This isn't your fault. I should've known better and come without you. Mello and I could've handled this."

"You're going to go to jail because of me." Guilt floods me. I've ruined another life and someone I love over a stupid mistake from my past.

"I'll be in and out, sugar. He's not going to charge me."

I gaze down, seeing the blood on his knuckles as he touches my face. I pull back, needing room to think and come to terms with what my stupidity caused.

Scooting back, I break the contact before he drops his hands. "I need time," I repeat, wondering how I fuck everything up.

Rocco would be better off without me. His life had been uncomplicated until I walked back in, little girl in tow, with a man after me who wanted nothing more than to track me down and probably hurt me again.

Beau groans, rolling over until his cheek rests against the bloody rocks and quiets again.

"He's fine," Rocco says, like somehow that makes

everything better.

"You turned into someone I didn't recognize." I rise to my feet, wiping the blood on my jeans.

Rocco's up and eye to eye with me a second later. "I won't apologize for what I did. I'd do it again if it meant protecting you and saving Adaline."

My belly flutters, but the fear of how quickly he snapped is still a visual I can't shake. "I just need time, Rocco. I'm still processing everything that happened. There was a gun on you."

He runs his fingers through his hair, the sun glinting off the wet blood on his hands. "And you stepped in front of that gun. He could've easily pulled the trigger. I wasn't going to let that happen. He's lucky he's still breathing. The fucker deserves to die."

My mouth falls open, and my eyes widen. "You wouldn't have killed him."

"If it means keeping you safe forever, I fuckin' would have. I protect what's mine and the people I love."

I back away when he reaches for me. "I'm driving back, following you alone in my own car."

"Darlin'," Carmello says, stepping to Rocco's side. "I'm taking Rocco's side on this one."

I throw up my hands. "Of course you are."

He shrugs. "Either way, no one's leaving here anytime soon. We have Beau and the police to deal with. We're stuck for a few hours minimum."

"Fucking great," I groan.

Before anyone can say anything else, a white SUV

with flashing lights, followed by an ambulance, pulls down the long driveway, stopping a dozen feet away.

A man with long legs unfolds himself from the vehicle, fixing his hat before making his way toward us. "Boys," he says, dipping his chin to Rocco and Carmello and then turns to me and does the same. "Ma'am."

"Curtis." Rocco lifts his chin. "I thought we wouldn't have to deal with this piece of shit, but here we are."

Curtis, the county sheriff, removes his sunglasses before dropping his arm, holding them between his fingers. "After your dad called, we had this place scouted out for days. Never saw the guy." His gaze moves toward the woods. "Probably hiding out in the woods, waiting to strike. Too much space to cover for our department."

"He came out of nowhere, but at least I was alone when he showed his face," Rocco explains, jostling back and forth on his feet like he's still burning through his anger.

Sheriff Curtis leans over, swiping the gun off the ground, quickly clearing it of any ammo. "Well, thank fuck no one was hurt. I'd have a hell of a time explaining that shit to your father, and the paperwork alone would've been a nightmare."

"Just kicked his ass," Rocco tells him.

"Good man," Curtis says, studying Beau as he moves around on the ground, moaning. "If anyone deserved an ass-whoopin', it was him."

"I had the gun, but I was late to the party and Rocco had it under control, or else you would've been chained to your desk all night with piles of that shit."

"Ma'am," Curtis says, turning to face me as I blink at the three of them, staying silent. "Are you all right?"

When I don't answer, he asks in a slower, softer tone, "Do you need the paramedics to look you over?"

"No," I whisper, suddenly finding my words. "I'm fine."

"Good thing the guys were with you. This man is a bad dude." The sheriff leans over, dropping his voice. "A really bad dude."

I peer down, staring at my feet. "I know."

"Do you now?" he asks.

I turn up my face, narrowing my eyes. "Um, he's hit me before. I'm well aware of what he's capable of, and I'm sure he didn't come here for a chat. He had a gun. He is, in fact, one hundred percent a bad dude."

Curtis eyes me. "You know of an Amanda Wallace?"

"No."

"She was his last woman, the one before you. Took out a restraining order against him."

"I'd believe that." After all the shit I went through with him, and now today, I'd believe he was capable of just about anything.

"When Mr. Caldo called me, I started to do some digging. It seems Ms. Wallace went missing last year. They're figuring this piece of shit is the one who made her vanish. Poof. Gone. 'Bout to have a real heart-to-heart with him after he's checked out by the medics and released into our custody."

"Oh my God. That's awful."

"Figurin' you were next to disappear, too, but—" he tips his head toward Rocco and Carmello "—seein' as you have these two in your life, I'd say you're about as safe as you can be. And with him—" he glances down until I only see the top of his hat "—being in jail probably for the rest of his breathing life, he'll never be a problem again."

"Okay," I whisper, trying to process everything. "Thank you."

"Carmello," the sheriff says, but my eyes are on Rocco. "I'll take your statement here and yours too, ma'am, but I'll need Rocco to hang back for a while."

"No problem."

"Take her home. I'll drive back in the morning," Rocco says, answering for me.

"Do you think you can talk now?" the sheriff asks me. "Ma'am?"

I drag my gaze from Rocco and face the sheriff. "Yes, sir. I can."

"Let's do this and get you on your way."

"Rebel," Rocco says, taking another step toward me, but I put up my hands when he reaches for me.

"Don't."

He backs away, dropping his arms to his sides. "This is fucked up," he mutters before I walk over to the police car and tell the sheriff everything that happened all the way back to when Beau and I first got together.

ROCCO

CARMELLO IS SOUND ASLEEP ON THE COUCH WHEN I walk through the front door. I kick off my boots and head toward the bedrooms, peeking inside and finding Rebel fast asleep in the spare bedroom.

Neither of those is a good sign.

I yank off my shirt, heading toward the shower before Rebel sees me and we have *the* talk.

I know I freaked her out, but I did it to protect her, and I'd do it again. She needs to understand I'm not the type of man that can just sit back and wait to see if the threat comes to fruition. I'm going to react, taking care of a situation before it turns uglier and I possibly lose the only person I've ever cared about.

I would never let that happen.

As long as I have air in my lungs and the ability to move, I'd kill a man before he could do the same to her or Addy.

Carmello's waiting for me in the kitchen when I'm

CHELLE BLISS

finished cleaning last night's mess off me. "You okay?" he asks, holding out a fresh cup of coffee.

I shrug as I take the cup, thankful he isn't entirely clueless in the kitchen. "I don't know. Is she okay?"

"She's confused and scared, Roc, but I think she'll be okay once she wakes up and realizes Beau and all his misery are in the past."

"Did I fuck up?"

He rests his ass against the counter, crossing his arms, thinking about his answer before he speaks. "I don't think so. I would've done the same in your shoes. It's how we were raised. Beau wasn't the type of man you were going to talk down. Pushing her out of the way may have been a little over the top, but…"

I take a sip before placing the mug on the counter, needing to talk through this before she wakes up. "She put herself in the line of fire. Was I just supposed to ask her to step aside so I could beat the piss out of him?"

"No, man. You were right, but the girl's been hurt. She's seen and experienced shit we could never imagine. She needs to separate all the bad shit from her past and realize you're not that type of man. You need to make sure she knows you'll always protect her and you'll never turn that big, bad energy on her. She needs to know she's safe, and she felt that way until she saw you lose your temper."

"Fuck," I hiss, shaking my head. "I'm sure I scared the shit out of her, but when I saw him with the gun and then she stepped in the middle, I just lost it."

Carmello places his hand on my shoulder. "You got

240

this. Tell her how you feel, and be open and honest with her. She'll listen. I heard her last night. She cried herself to sleep. She's torn and needs you to help her make that final leap."

"Damn it," I mutter as my stomach knots. "I should've come back earlier."

"You love her?" my brother asks me, staring me in the eye.

"Completely."

"You tell her that."

I shake my head.

"Tell her, Rocco. Don't wait. Do it today. Love makes us do crazy shit, but she needs to hear those words and know you mean them. A girl like her needs safety, security, and assurance."

"How do you know all this shit when you can't seem to stay in a relationship longer than five fucking minutes?"

"Life's too short to get tied down. There's too much fun to be had and too much pleasure to give to only one person for the rest of my life."

I shake my head, laughing. "The universe is going to play a wicked trick on you someday."

He shrugs. "Doubtful."

"Whatever you say, brother. Thank you for last night."

He nods. "I'm out. Got shit to do and broads to bang. You take care of that one. I already talked to Mom, and you have until tonight before she brings Adaline back. Make good use of that time."

I grab him before he has a chance to walk away and pull him into a bear hug. "I don't know what I'd do without you."

"You couldn't survive without me," he teases, hugging me just as tight before giving my back a light tap.

He's right, though.

I haven't had a moment of my life without him, and I'm not sure how I'd live if he weren't somewhere nearby. We came out of the womb together, but some-day, one of us will go before the other. That is a thought I try very hard not to entertain because it brings me too much pain.

"Love you, man," I tell him as he starts to walk toward the door.

He pulls on his boots and looks over his shoulder before he reaches for the knob. "Love you too."

I take another sip of my coffee, knowing what I have to do and unable to wait. I make my way to Rebel's room, finding her curled in a ball in the middle of the bed.

I slide in behind her, my chest bare but my bottom half covered in my favorite gray sweats. She melts into me as my arm settles around her middle, her back to my front.

"Morning, sugar," I whisper in her ear, smelling the sweetness of her shampoo and reveling in the warmth of her body.

Her hand moves to mine as I cover her belly, tight-ening my embrace. She doesn't say anything as we lie there, her drifting in and out of sleep and me doing everything I can to keep from being pulled under myself.

"They let you go?" she whispers, still facing the other direction.

"No reason to keep me."

"I thought they might arrest you too."

Using my hand, I turn her flat on her back to see her face. "They weren't going to keep me, Rebel. I was protecting you, and around these parts, that's what a man does when he loves someone. Beau's gone. He's alive, but he'll never feel the sun on his face again. Never know the love of a good woman and have the ability to fuck someone up the way he fucked you up and the countless other women before you."

She blinks slowly, her face soft from sleep. "When you love someone?" she repeats like she didn't hear anything else I said.

"I love you, Rebel," I whisper, staring down into her beautiful, deep-blue eyes. "And if saving your life this weekend, making sure Beau is behind bars for the rest of your life, makes you walk away, at least I can sleep at night, knowing you don't ever have to look over your shoulder again."

"You love me?" she says again, this time a little louder, her body moving closer.

I move my palm to her face, cradling her cheek. "I've loved you since the moment I laid eyes on you."

"I love you too," she whispers, curling into my chest to face me. "So damn much it scares me."

"I'd never hurt you," I promise her, stroking her cheek softly.

"I know you wouldn't."

"When you stepped in front of that gun, I panicked, Rebel. I lost my shit, imagining him shooting you and having to watch you die in my arms like Carrie did. I shouldn't have pushed you, sugar, but it was the only thing I could think to do to move you out of his range."

She reaches up, placing her hand on my neck. "I was scared he was going to shoot you. I would've gone with him if it meant you'd be okay."

"Don't do that shit. Not ever. You have a child to raise and love. I'll take that bullet all day long and die knowing Adaline has a mommy to come home to."

"I won't."

I press on her neck, tipping her lips up to mine, staring at her. "You need to know that I'll never hurt you. Beau had it coming, but I'll never lift a hand to hurt you. I don't care how mad you make me, I'll never lay a hand on you."

"I know," she says, stroking my neck. "I've never felt safer than I do with you, Rocco."

"You're always safe with me, love. Always and forever." I lean forward, putting my mouth on hers, taking what I've wanted and craved for the last ten years.

I move on top of her, settling between her legs, kissing her harder and deeper than before. "Marry me," I murmur between breaths.

Her eyes fly open, meeting mine. "What?" she whispers.

"Marry me, Rebel. I'm sick of waiting. Ten years have passed, and now that you're here again, I'm never letting you go."

She stares at me, her eyes searching mine, and for a second, I think she's going to say no. "Yes," she tells me. "I want nothing more."

I'm overjoyed. Happiest I've ever been in my life to know she feels the same and has agreed to be mine forever.

Her hands find the waistband of my sweats, yanking them down until her feet take over, pushing them to my ankles. "Make love to me," she says against my mouth. "Make me yours. I want to feel owned."

Fuck me.

She has no idea what those words do or mean to me, but I'm going to give it to her slow and deep, rocking into her until she's moaning my name.

And I do that after her hands wrap around my cock, guiding me to her pussy. I push inside, our mouths still locked, and slide my hands under her ass, keeping her where I want her.

The feeling is joyous.

A union of souls and bodies. This is where I was always meant to be and where we are destined to end up, even if the path to this point was long and completely fucked up.

Rebel Bishop is finally mine, and I can't wait to tell the world.

"SAY THAT AGAIN." My mother grips the countertop like she is about to fall over or faint. "I don't think I heard you right."

"We're getting married, Ma."

Dad smiles from behind her, wrapping his arms around her waist to give her strength. "Happy, baby?" he asks her.

"Don't tease me. I'm too old for you to play games with my heart like that, Rocco. So help me God, I'll…"

"We are," Rebel adds, stopping my mother from her theatrics and threats of stroking out on me if I was pulling her leg.

Ma blinks, placing her hand over my father's at her waist. "You're getting married?" she asks, as if she needs to say the words out loud to finally comprehend.

"Yeah, Ma. I asked Rebel this morning, and she said yes."

Ma leans back, letting my father take her weight. "Thank you, Jesus," she whispers.

"She's very dramatic," I explain to Rebel, which gets me a hip nudge and a wrinkled nose.

"You have three boys come out of your vagina and raise them, trying to keep the fools alive, and find yourself not being dramatic when you're older," Ma says.

I laugh. "Not possible since I don't have the parts, but we have a little girl, and if she's anything like her mother, Lord help me."

Ma smiles, liking the sound of that. "I have two girls

now. Two," she repeats, wiping at her eyes like she's crying.

Total drama queen.

Rebel squeezes my hand, and I squeeze hers back before pulling her against me and throwing my arm over her shoulder.

"When's the wedding?" Mom asks, her eyes moving between Rebel and me.

Rebel peers up at me, her hand over my heart and her other hand resting on the top of my ass, waiting for me to answer that one.

"Ma, it's been a few hours. We have no idea. Give us a few weeks to figure some shit out. As soon as we know, you'll know."

My dad gives her middle a tug, and she tips her head back, staring at him. "Fine," she mutters, pretending to be sad, but she's about to burst at the seams.

He's trying to reel her in and keep her ass in check, something he's done a moderately decent job of over the years, but this event is on a whole new level, as will be her celebration.

"I have to call my mother," she says, and that means it's about to hit the Gallo newswire, spreading the information across the family. It'll break the laws of physics, traveling faster than the speed of light. "She's going to be over the freaking moon excited."

"Here we go," I mumble, bracing myself for the barrage of calls and messages that will be hitting my phone within the hour.

Mom steps out of Dad's arms and grabs Rebel's

hand, pulling her away from me. "Come sit with me, and we can FaceTime her together and share the good news."

Rebel glances over her shoulder, and I give her a chin lift, letting her know it's okay. It isn't a secret we were ever going to be able to keep, and my grandmother will be ridiculously happy.

There's nothing the Gallos love more than a wedding and the possibility of more humans joining the family tree. And that includes Adaline. She is now one of us, along with Rebel, but they had been brought into the fold the moment they stepped foot inside my grandmother's house, even if I never put a ring on Rebel's finger.

Dad steps forward, placing his hand on my shoulder. "You look happy," he says, his eyes sweeping over my face, studying me intently like he has for years.

"I am, Dad. For the first time in a decade, I feel at peace."

"I'm proud of you."

"That means a lot."

"And the club?" he asks, going somewhere I haven't put a ton of thought into.

I shrug. "Haven't been there in a while and don't plan on going back unless Rebel wants to explore that side of herself."

"You're a man of certain tastes, and those don't require a specific set of four walls for you to embrace that side of yourself."

I nod. "I feel like I finally have control back of my entire life. It's an odd and wonderful feeling."

His hand tightens on my shoulder. "Your other half was missing, and you tried to fill that emptiness, using whatever control you could find to do it. But now that it's back—*she's* back—you're at peace and complete, son. I only hope you're ready for the insanity you just put into motion."

"I think I am." I grimace, remembering Gigi's, Lily's, Tamara's, and Nick's weddings and the stupidity that ran rampant through the family until the big day.

"Brace for it."

"Braced," I tell him before moving in for a hug, something we do often in this family.

My dad, for being as big and badass as he is, isn't above showing affection and letting us know we matter and are loved.

He has been my role model my entire life, and I've looked up to him for the way he loves my mom and us. We are his everything, and I am about to have mine.

We walk into the living room as Adaline crawls into my mom's lap, putting her face as close as she can to the phone. "Oh, it's Nonna," Adaline says, making goofy faces. "Hi!"

"Hi, baby," Grandma says back.

"We just wanted you to know, Ma," my mother tells my grandma. "We knew you'd be happy."

"Happy about what?" Adaline asks, looking at my mother and then to hers.

Rebel smiles, running her fingers across Adaline's cheek. "Rocco and Mommy are going to get married."

Adaline's eyes get huge, and her mouth gapes open. "You are?"

Rebel nods. "Yeah, bug. What do you think?"

"Does that mean Izzy's going to be my nonna too?" Adaline asks, looking right at my mother, cementing her position in the family forever.

My mom's face changes, scrunching up, and I know what's coming.

"Ah, fuck," Dad mutters, and he knows too.

Ma covers her mouth with both hands as tears start to form in her eyes. "I'm going to have girls. Girls," she whispers.

"Nonna?" Adaline asks again.

My mom wraps her arms around Adaline, burying her face in the crook of her neck. "Yeah, baby. You can call me whatever you want, but I'm going to get to be your grandma forever and ever."

Dad puts his hand on my shoulder as he stands behind me. "It was a good run, but it was bound to end sometime."

Adaline shifts, turning her body into my mom and wrapping her arms around Ma's neck. "I'm so excited. This is the best day ever."

The kid is right. It is the best day of my life so far.

2 2

REBEL

SIX MONTHS LATER

My feet stop moving as soon as we round the corner and the entire backyard comes into view. It isn't just because the yard has been decked out, looking more beautiful than I've ever seen it, with white twinkling lights hanging from the trees and lanterns scattered about, but because of the number of people standing around, laughing, talking, and dancing.

"It's okay, sugar. It's just friends and family," Rocco says with his hand on my lower back, giving me a moment to soak it all in.

"I thought I'd met them all," I whisper.

He laughs. "You only met the Florida Gallo side of the family. There's a whole different Gallo side from Chicago and Caldos from Miami."

My gaze drifts across the crowd, soaking in all the handsome, broad-shouldered men, covered in muscles, and also looking like sin. Gallo and Caldo blood, for sure. The women are just as stunning as the men, but far louder, given the way the voices carry across the yard.

"Mommy," Adaline whispers, leaning across Rocco's body to tap me on the shoulder.

I turn my head, my mouth still open and in complete shock.

"Can I go play?"

I nod, smiling at my little girl. "Do not leave the yard."

"Well, duh," she says, having found an attitude since she started school here.

She instantly fit in, and having a small army of Gallo kids at the school helped. She wasn't an outsider on the first day, instead surrounded by friendly faces who pulled her into the fold and showed her the ropes.

"Love you, Daddy," she whispers, and she kisses Rocco's cheek before kicking her legs and wiggling down his body.

She is gone before I have a chance to register what she just said.

"Did she just…" Rocco's voice breaks, and his eyes move to where Adaline is running. "She said that, didn't she? I didn't hear shit?"

"You did not hear shit. She called you Daddy."

"I'm…" He pauses, putting his hands to his lips, and his eyes start to swirl with emotion. "I just…"

I tighten my arm around his back. "She loves you just like her mother."

"My girls," he whispers, smiling.

A small woman with a cane steps forward, shorter

than most and hair as dark as mine. "Lemme get a good look at her," she says, motioning for me to bend over and bring my face closer.

"My dad's mom," Rocco whispers in my ear.

I smile, letting her study my features. "You're going to give me stunningly beautiful great-grandbabies," she whispers, touching my cheek gently. "Just as Izzy did with the boys, but you will only have girls."

"Fucking hell," Rocco mutters, straightening his back when she turns her gaze on him with one eyebrow raised.

"Girls are a blessing, my boy," she says to him. "You will never go hungry when surrounded by women."

"But I can also go to jail, Gram. Come on. One boy, at least?"

She shakes her head. "You're surrounded by pink."

"Damn it."

I peer up at him, still hunched over in front of her, and smile with a shrug.

"She has some magic old-school voodoo in her. She's never wrong when it comes to things like this."

I jerk when his grandmother places her hand on my stomach when I'm not looking.

"There's one in there already."

I laugh, thinking she's cute and also very wrong. There's no baby growing inside me or else I'd know…wouldn't I?

Rocco looks at me, his eyes dipping to where his

grandmother's hand is splayed across my belly. "Are you…"

"No."

"She's never wrong, Rebel," he tells me.

"There's a first time for everything," I whisper, hoping she doesn't hear me.

"I'm not wrong. I can feel her spirit."

"Ma," Rocco's mother says, coming to rescue us, taking his grandma by the shoulders and guiding her away from us.

I straighten my back, but I can't stop myself from staring as the two disappear into the crowd. "You think she's right?" I ask Rocco, not giving him my eyes.

"Not this time." He presses his hand against my back, turning my front to his. "But I can't say I don't like the idea of my baby growing in your belly."

"Our baby," I remind him, rubbing my nose against the whiskers and groping his ass. "Our little girl."

He grunts, moving his lips to mine, and kisses me long and deep in front of everyone. I pull back, knowing I want more than I can have right now, and by his taking my mouth, he's only making me want it more.

"Rocco," a woman says and clears her throat. "Sorry to interrupt."

We turn, my one hand still on his ass and his at the small of my back as I resume the spot I've grown accustomed to under his arm.

"Tater Tot?" Rocco whispers, squinting.

The young woman nods. "It's me, cousin. I wouldn't

miss this weekend for the world. This wedding is going to be the shit."

Rocco laughs, only releasing me to wrap his arms around her. "Holy fuck," he howls. "You fucking grew up."

"Tits and all," she says as he pulls away, smiling the biggest and most beautiful smile. "Drove Dad and Mom crazy as fuck, too. It's been a wild ride."

"Tate, this is my fiancée, Rebel. Rebel, this is my cousin Tate."

"Hi," I say softly.

"Hiya," she replies, pushing her hair over her shoulder.

"You doing good?" he asks her.

"Great. I mean…that's my flavor of the month," she says next, pointing to a big guy covered in tats, wearing a cut, and standing next to Mammoth.

"Oh boy," I whisper, figuring that's what she meant by a wild ride and her parents not being overly excited about it.

"His name is Rowdy."

"I'm sure it is," I mutter, giving her a wink when she brings her eyes to me.

"He's the best."

"Uh-huh," Rocco mumbles.

"Anyway, thought I'd say hi before I lose you to the family. I better get back to Rowdy." She smiles, touching my hand. "You know how men are."

I smile back, but I don't know what she means.

Rocco isn't like the other men I've known. "I do," I lie. "It was great meeting you."

"You too," she says with a wave. "Love ya, cuz."

"Angelo and Tilly have to be losing their shit."

"I'd lose mine," I tell him honestly. "All that tits, ass, hair, and a badass biker dude. I'd have no shit left."

Rocco's body shakes. "You're too much. Look at Mammoth. Dude loves my cousin like crazy. Best thing to ever happen to her crazy-as-fuck ass. Don't judge a book by its cover, sugar."

"You're right. He might be the nicest guy ever."

"Let's not kid ourselves. But he might be good for her. Who the hell knows? It's been years since I've seen Tate. She had a rough patch for a bit, but she seems to have worked her shit out."

"Rough patch?" I ask, my eyes moving back to the happy-looking girl clinging to her biker man.

"She loves Angelo and Tilly, but Tilly isn't her bio mom. She died when Tate was really little, and she had some shit to work through in her teenage years. Trauma from that loss she hadn't quite gotten out of her system."

"How awful." I frown, seeing the younger woman in a new light. She was finding herself, searching for her identity at a time that wasn't easy for any hormonal teenager, especially one who'd lost her mom.

"Cancer sucks, baby."

"It does."

"Anyway, enough sad shit. This is our rehearsal dinner and party. You ready to meet everyone else?" he asks me, pulling me tighter against his side and brushing his lips over my temple.

"I don't know. There're a lot of people. Give me the rundown and know I won't remember anyone's name tomorrow."

He chuckles against my skin. "The families have split, which makes it easier, like some invisible force has moved them apart. To the left are the Chicago Gallos. Solid people. Hardworking and own a family bar on the South Side. My grandpa's brother's kids and grandkids. Santino's his name. Total dog and spent some time in prison for some bullshit he pulled that wasn't on the up-and-up."

"Why are you talking like we're in a Godfather movie?"

"'Cause that side of the family, at least Santino, is like something out of *the Godfather*. He and my grand-father hated each other for a long time, but they buried the hatchet when I was little. Santino and Betty, she's the redhead," he tells me, pointing at a drop-dead gorgeous woman who doesn't look old enough to be a grandma, with the brightest red hair I've ever seen. "They had four kids. Three boys and a girl. Daphne, Angelo, Lucio, and Vinnie." He moves his finger with each name, but I'm already confused. "Vinnie was a star in the NFL, played for the Bears, so of course the family thought he was the shit. Didn't matter that his wife wrote the spiciest stories and even had a movie made from one of her books."

My mouth drops open. "No shit?"

"No lie."

"Wow."

"We don't see them often, but when we do, it's the best fucking time."

"Good to know."

"You know the middle group. The regular crowd from Sunday, plus a few extra friends thrown in from my dad's work."

"Yeah, baby." I place my head against his shoulder, scanning the crowd.

"And that side," he says, pointing to the right, "is my father's family. If you thought the Gallos were loud and nosy, you haven't seen anything yet."

"Oh boy."

"Yep. You need a few drinks before soaking them in."

I point off to the corner, a group of rough-looking men along with Bear. "Who are they?"

"ALFA guys. My dad and Uncle Thomas own the company, and they work there. Bounty hunting, security, investigations. All kinds of crazy, off-the-wall, dangerous shit."

My eyes widen. "Your dad owns something like that?"

"He and Uncle Thomas used to work for the government, working undercover on sting operations. They said they left that bullshit to make their own money without being told what to do by the big guy. So, they did, and that's their team. Solid dudes."

"They look like it," I tease, eyeing the ragtag group of burly men.

"Come on. I want to show you off, sugar."

I like that. He is proud of me. No one has ever been proud of me. Not Collin, certainly not Beau, and no one in my family.

For the first time, I feel like I have it all, including a man and a family who love and embrace me and my little girl. Tomorrow, it will be official. Rocco and I will be husband and wife. I can't wait to walk down the aisle, heading straight to my future.

I PACE the tiny room tucked away down a hallway in the church.

"Girl, calm down. You're like a caged animal," Tamara says to me, sitting on the couch and adjusting her cleavage. "No sense in worrying unless you want out."

I stop walking, turning to her, shaking out my hands. "I do not want out. I've never wanted anything more, but I'm never this lucky."

The floor always falls out from under me, and I expect the same to happen today. Something has to go wrong, but so far, it's been smooth sailing. It is like the universe isn't against me for the first time in my life.

Gigi grabs my shoulders, her face soft and sweet. "Just breathe and remember, one foot in front of the other. It's a happy day and not one to be busy with worry. Rocco loves you, yeah?"

"Yes."

"You love him?"

"More than anything."

"Then walk toward him knowing you're going where you are meant to be. I was nervous before my wedding, but as soon as I stepped foot into the church, everything vanished besides Pike. When he saw me and his face lit up, I glided down that aisle as if I were carried by some invisible force."

"Me too," Tamara adds. "Everyone is nervous beforehand, and there's no reason for it."

"There are going to be so many people in there," I tell them. "So many and no one on my side of the church."

"Both sides are packed. Caldos and Chicago on one side and the rest of us on the other. You are not alone in this," Lily says, coming to stand next to Gigi in front of me.

The door opens, and Izzy steps inside, looking stunning in a red dress. "Can I have a minute?" she says, looking at Tamara, Gigi, Jo, and Lily.

"Have fun," Gigi says, winking at me before she peels away, taking the other girls with her.

"Adaline okay?" I ask her as she closes the door.

"She's fine, dear. James has her, and they're like two peas in a pod."

They took to Adaline like she was their own blood,

keeping her as many weekends as we'd allow. And since we were new, that was often.

Izzy's eyes roam over me, sweeping across my dress before coming back to my face. She closes the space between us with a smile on her face. "You're absolutely beautiful, Rebel. The most stunning bride I've ever seen."

"Thank you, Izzy," I say, but I know it's something everyone says to every bride, even though they're all as equally and uniquely pretty as the others.

She reaches out, taking my hands in hers, and gives my fingers a light squeeze. "Mom," she whispers.

I blink, staring back at her. "Mom what?"

"I want you to call me Mom. You're marrying my son, and that makes you my daughter and that little girl out there my grandbaby. No more Izzy or Mrs. Caldo, only Mom. You can say no and it'll hurt like hell, but it would make my heart happy to hear you use that word."

I blink again, feeling the water filling my eyes. "Mom," I whisper, the word foreign on my tongue.

Izzy smiles, reaching up to cradle my face in the palms of her hands. "You're ours now just as much as we're yours. You will never be alone again. Never have to worry about anything when you have the power and safety of this family behind you. You aren't just marrying my son. You're solidifying your bond with the entire family."

A tear slides down my face, feeling the words deeply as she speaks them. "I don't know what to say. I haven't had a family since…"

My mother was just a passing memory, and my aunt was nothing but a bitch. It has been more than ten years since I've spoken to her, and I have no plans of changing that.

"Family isn't always where you are born, dear. You're a Caldo now—and a Gallo, even if not by name. You've brought my boy back, given him the light back in his eyes that I haven't seen in a decade. You've given me far more than I could ever give you, but I will spend the rest of my life making sure you know just how much you're wanted, loved, and appreciated, along with that sweet little grand-baby of mine, sitting on her grandpa's lap right now, talking his ear off about the different princesses."

I smile, imagining James keeping his calm as Adaline prattles on about crowns, colors, and castles. "She loves you all just as deeply as I do," I tell Izzy. "And I do, Mom."

Izzy's face softens again, and she sniffles. "Now, no more of this talk. We're going to ruin our makeup." She lifts her fingers toward my eyes, brushing away the tears that have fallen free. "It's a happy day."

"The happiest day of my life," I whisper.

"I'm going to go rescue James, but he'll be back here in a minute to walk you down the aisle. Rocco's already at the altar."

I reach out and pull her into an embrace, careful not to wrinkle her dress or my own. "Thank you for loving me like no one else has ever loved me. Words aren't enough."

She pulls back and shakes her head. "We love you and always will," she says before releasing me. "The best part of your life is about to start, sweetheart. Just remember, you deserve every ounce of joy that's about to come your way."

I smile, holding back any more words because I'll end up with my face scrunched up and in ugly-cry hell, tears streaming down my face and taking my makeup with them.

As soon as she's gone, I start pacing again, burning off the nervous energy I can't shake. I didn't give my first wedding a second thought, but I knew it wasn't for love. We went to the courthouse, sealing the agreement quickly with zero fanfare. I didn't have dreams of love and happiness, only security and safety for myself and our little girl.

But with Rocco, it is different. This marriage is about happiness and a future we can build, growing old together surrounded by Adaline and hopefully more children and, eventually, our own grandchildren.

There's a light rap at the door before Mr. Caldo stands in the doorway, filling it up entirely. "Ready?" he asks, his eyes soaking me in for the first time, in my long white dress with layer upon layer of lace.

"I am." I swallow and move toward my bouquet, but he gets there first.

"Couldn't be happier today, baby girl." He holds the bouquet out to me, and I take it, but I keep my eyes trained on him. "Waited my whole life for a daughter and got a granddaughter as a bonus. Happiest man in the world. That's what I am today."

"Me too," I say with a smile, pushing back the tears that are once again threatening to take up residence in my eyes.

"You ready? Rocco's waiting, and so is the entire family."

I nod and blow out a breath. "I am, Mr...."

He shakes his head. "Dad, baby. Call me Dad."

Do not cry.

Do not cry.

Fuck.

I am going to cry.

"I get to walk you down the aisle today, something I never thought I'd be able to do, seeing as I have three boys. But I'm that man, the one whose arm you're going to be on, taking you to my son to create a new family. Give me that title, and I promise to earn it every single day."

"You already have," I whisper, not trusting my voice. "You already have, Dad."

He smiles, moving his hands to mine and squeezing them lightly before offering me his elbow.

I take it, gazing up at him, seeing the same beautiful features on his face that I see in Rocco's. "Let's do this," I tell him with a quick nod.

The hallway leading to the church is empty except for the two of us and the sound of the music coming from inside the chapel.

When we stop in front of the doors, waiting for them

to open, he turns his eyes to me again and says, "Izzy and I were married here. She walked down the same aisle you will. Happiest day of my life. I figure my son is going to feel the same way I did, watching his future walk toward him. Keep your eyes on him and step into it, baby."

"Step into it," I repeat as the doors swing open, the people inside stand, and my gaze moves down the aisle to where Rocco is standing on the altar.

His shoulders are square, back straight, eyes only on me. My belly flutters, and for a second, I don't move, too winded by the handsomeness of the man and the dumb luck that I am about to marry him.

My feet only move forward when James takes a step, taking me with him. I do as he said, keeping my eyes on Rocco, our gazes locked. No one else matters. It is only him and me as I march down the aisle, leaving my past behind me and looking forward to whatever the future holds.

Rocco's smile only grows wider the closer I get, his eyes never leaving mine, saying so much without ever speaking a word.

James stops at the bottom of the steps, keeping me there instead of letting me close the last few feet between his son and me.

"Who here gives this woman to be wed to this man?" the priest asks.

"I do," James says in a deep tone before turning to me and whispering, "Love ya, kid. You got this."

The entire family makes me feel like anything is

possible, but no one more than the man I am about to marry.

Then he reaches out his hand, and I slide mine into his, letting him pull me up the stairs. I don't hear a thing the priest says because I am too busy staring at the man in front of me decked out in a suit, looking more handsome than I would have ever thought possible.

Behind him are his brothers, Trace and Carmello, along with his cousins, Pike, Jett, Nick, and Mammoth. They are all the most beautiful sight in the world. All there for us, showing their support, becoming part of our union and our future too.

"I love you," Rocco mouths as I stare at him, unable to look anywhere else.

"Love you too," I mouth back, knowing whatever lies in front of us is nothing but wonderful.

EPILOGUE

Rocco
One Year Later

CARMELLO WALKS INTO INKED, HIS HAIR MESSY AND IN
the same clothes as yesterday.

"Rough night?" Rebel asks him before he can blow
by her at the front desk, where she's working on the
schedule.

"Oh, it was rough, darlin', but not in the bad kind of
way." He stops near the edge of the desk and takes a
knee, looking at our daughter fast asleep in the baby
carrier. "I need to get me one of these."

All my uncles along with Mom have officially
retired, handing over the shop to us kids to run. That
frees them up to watch the grandkids, and they couldn't
be happier. Neither could we because we have unlimited
freedom to do with the shop as we wish.

Rebel turns, resting her hip against the counter,

staring at him as he touches the baby's cheek with the backs of his knuckles. "You may have a few out there already," she teases him.

"I have no kids. Trust me, if I did have one out there, I'd know."

"Would you?" Rebel questions him, riding his ass like she's been his sister his entire life. "I mean, I'm sure the girls don't sleep around and could pinpoint the daddy without a problem."

"Are you saying I sleep with easy chicks?"

She laughs. "Mello, you are the easy one in this situation. How many women do you think you've slept with in the last year?"

There's a long pause. "Fuck, I don't know."

I laugh and continue prepping my station, shaking my head at the stupidity of my brother.

"Give me an estimate."

"There are 365 days in a year, and I go out pretty often, and this year was one for the record books."

"You're such a whore," she tells him, kneeling next to him as he continues staring at our little girl, unable to come up with a solid number.

"Someday, one of them is going to walk through the door and surprise your ass."

He shakes his head and grunts. "Not happening. I always wear protection."

"Always?" Rebel raises an eyebrow, twisting her lips, totally judging him on his whorish behavior.

"Like, ninety percent of the time. Sometimes we

party a little too hard, and shit gets crazy. You know how it is."

"Yeah, when I was a teenager, dumbass. You're thirty. Keep that shit under wraps."

"He wants to be free," Carmello tells her, and I have to bite my lip to stop myself from busting out laughing.

"He's truly an idiot," Gigi says from the station next to me. "I don't know how he gets so much pussy."

"He drowns himself in it so he doesn't have to deal with any feelings, and he's fucking good-looking."

"You only say that because you share his face."

"Yep. I know what this face can get a man."

She rolls her eyes. "You have a better personality."

"I do now, but I was a miserable prick, and the chicks still wanted me. He's the fun one—fucked up in the head —but the fun one, and they all want a piece of his dick, hoping their pussy is the magical one that sticks."

"Men are dumb, but women are dumber," she whispers, covering her station in plastic before our doors open for the day.

"I heard chicks like men with babies. Think I could take Liv with me one night?"

Rebel blinks, but she doesn't move otherwise or speak. She only glares, something I've seen thrown my way more than once, and it's not a good feeling.

"I'll take that as a no."

"You are not taking my daughter to shop for pussy."

He throws his hands up and rises from the floor. "She'd be safe."

Rebel stands too, her eyes still narrowed. "She is not a pussy magnet."

"How do I attract the good ones unless I have a baby at my side?"

Rebel crosses her arms, cocking one shoulder. "Why don't you try treating them like they matter and they're more than just a quick fuck."

He blinks, staring back at her. "I treat every single one of them like a queen. They never walk away without an orgasm."

"Well, aren't you Prince fucking Charming."

"You're an idiot!" Gigi yells out, to which Lily pops her head out of the piercing room, nodding her agreement.

"I can hear your dumb ass back here and, cousin, I love you, man, but you know nothing about women. You want to catch a good one, don't try to get in their pants within the first hour."

"They want in mine," he argues like it somehow makes it better.

"Go somewhere else besides a bar or a club. Try hanging out at the library or a bookstore."

He jerks his head back. "What? You're fucking with me."

"If she's shaking her ass at a club, she only wants to give you her ass. Strike up a conversation with a chick looking at a book and pay attention to her mind, and that pussy might stick," Rebel tells him.

I love the way she talks to him, giving him the advice he's always needed but never paid attention to.

He respects Rebel, though. She is about the only person he ever takes advice from, and he tries his best to follow through, even if he inevitably fails.

"Win her mind, and you'll get her heart."

"So, no sex on the first date?"

Rebel's eyes flash. "No. Maybe a kiss on the cheek, but anything more has to wait."

The words rock him back on his heels. "How is that even possible? I'm a man."

She rolls her eyes and groans.

"Lord bless her for trying with that one," Gigi mutters. "I'd have given up long ago. He's a lost soul, drowning in useless pussy."

"He'll grow up eventually."

"Sure, whatever," she mumbles.

"Lily!" Carmello yells from the front of the shop.

A second later, Lily pokes her head out again and says, "What?"

"I need you," he tells her, glancing toward her room. "I need you to teach me how to talk to someone like you."

She blinks, her jaw set hard. "Excuse me? Someone like me?"

"A bookish chick. A nerdy girl," he explains.

I cover my face, laughing because he's about to get his ass whooped by the nerdy girl. She doesn't play, and sometimes he forgets her daddy taught her how to take down any man in only a few quick moves. She may be little, but she knows how to use her power, and she uses that shit wisely.

Lily raises her chin, stalking in his direction, cheeks tinged pink. "You want to say that again because I'm not sure I heard you right."

He swallows, giving her a smile, tucking his hands in his pockets. "I want to find a good girl, and you're the best one I know."

Nice save.

He is a smooth talker and fast on his feet when he isn't thirsting after ass.

She eyes him, but he holds her stare. "Please, Lily. Take pity on my sinful soul."

She shakes her head and covers her face, mumbling into her palm.

"Do you want me to be alone forever?"

"Oh, for fuck's sake," Rebel mutters, going back to the books. "The man is ridiculous."

Lily sighs. "I'll teach you everything you need to know, but I need you to promise me something first."

"What?" he asks, taking a step toward her.

"Promise me you'll use the knowledge for good and not to literally tap into a whole new market."

He moves his fingers over his heart. "I swear. Scout's honor."

"You were never a scout."

"I know, but it sounded good."

"Forget it." She waves her hand at him, going to turn her back.

"Wait." He reaches out, grabbing her by the elbow. "Please. I beg you. I'll do whatever you want."

"What the fuck is happening?" Pike says, walking

into the work area from the back door, seeing the exchange between Lily and Carmello.

"He wants help looking for his wife."

Pike moves his hand across his hair, confusion on his face. "What wife?"

"He says he's going to turn over a new leaf. He wants to settle down and have babies."

Pike bursts into laughter and collapses back into his chair. "This should be fun."

"You got that right," I tell him. "It's going to make for an interesting time at the shop."

"I see a lot of misery in all of our futures," Pike adds. "Lots of fucking misery."

"Fine." Lily blows out a breath and rubs her temples. "We'll start tomorrow, but the moment you fuck up, it's over."

"Teach me all your womanly wisdom." He smiles and gives her a wink. "I'm a sponge."

"You need a sponge. I can smell the sex on you, and the yesterday's-clothes look…not good. We have a lot of work ahead of us."

"I'm going to make you proud," he tells her. "You'll all see. I'm about to find me a woman."

Those words are meant for all of us, and by the look on his face, I'd say he was serious, but that doesn't stop us from laughing.

Whatever is about to happen, I am going to enjoy every freaking second of it.

"Honey," Rebel calls, walking my way. "Remember we have the lawyer at three."

"Got it," I tell her, wrapping my arms around her waist and pulling her in for a kiss. "Couldn't forget it. Been waiting a year for this."

Today, I am adopting Adaline, officially making her mine. My life is perfectly complete, something I never thought possible two years ago.

"I'll grab Adaline from school and meet you there if you run over with your customers. You're booked pretty tight."

"I'll be done and go with you. We do this, we do it as a family and not separately. I want to walk through those doors with my girls on my arms."

"I love you," she whispers.

"I love you too," I murmur against her lips before taking her mouth, pressing mine to hers and kissing her deeply.

Rebel
One month later

"WHAT'S THIS?" Rocco asks, staring at the large box on the coffee table.

"A present." I chew on my thumbnail, watching him as he moves his eyes from the box to me.

"Did I forget what day it is?"

I shift my weight from one foot to another, trying to control my excitement. "No, baby. You didn't forget anything. This is a gift for the two of us. We have the house to ourselves, and I've been holding on to this for a while, waiting for the right moment."

He sits down, his eyes trained on the package with a look of confusion on his face. "I feel like I'm missing something."

"You aren't," I tell him as I kneel on the other side of the table, keeping my gaze pinned on him. "This is just a little something fun for us."

His head comes up and his eyes meet mine. "Fun?"

"I have to keep you on your toes." I bite my lip, holding back my smile.

I've been a hot mess for the last hour, impatiently waiting for him to get home from work. I left early, dropped the girls off at his parents', and walked in the door to prep for tonight.

Rocco had been a man of specific tastes before I'd met him again. Tastes he's buried and sworn he doesn't miss. He's been good at suppressing that side of himself, but I know he still craves part of his former life. And although I haven't had many romantic role models in my life, I know enough about human behavior to understand someone can only suppress a part of themselves for so long before they either find themselves unhappy in their day-to-day life or walking out the door to find what they've been missing.

I know my husband loves me. I've never doubted the feelings he has for me a single day over the last year. But I also know I want my husband happy and to be himself too.

I've spent time studying everything I can about his

particular sexual proclivities, even going as far as to talk with Mammoth and Izzy, separately, of course—which was totally awkward, but necessary.

"Just open it," I tell him, pushing the package closer to him and fighting the urge to tear it open myself. "You'll like it."

He makes quick work of the wrapping paper, exposing the plain cardboard box underneath. He snaps his eyes to mine, brow furrowing, still unsure of what's inside or why I bought it.

"You're not this slow at Christmas," I tease him, dying a little inside every minute he draws this out.

"I'm expecting gifts then," he says as he pops the tape running across the seam of the box. "Now, I feel like something's going to jump out, like a puppy."

"Not even remotely close and it's more a gift for the two of us."

He raises an eyebrow. "Something for the two of us?"

I nod, unable to hide my excitement, and somehow, I tamp down the nervous energy running through my system.

He glances around, finally realizing we're alone. "Where's the girls?"

"Your parents' for the night."

A smile spreads across his face. "We have the place to ourselves for the night?"

"We do." I smile.

He smirks. "That is present enough. Some alone naked time with my wife is enough."

"I'm about to make your night then, baby, but you're fucking torturing me with the speed at which you're moving."

He laughs as he peels back the flaps of the box, exposing the tissue paper I placed over the contents to add even more suspense. To my surprise, he doesn't take out the top layer of paper before reaching inside and feeling around.

His hand stills as his eyes widen. "What did you buy?"

I chew on my lips again and lift my eyebrows. "Some things to make tonight really interesting."

He lifts his arm, and the first item out of the box and in his hand is a cute leather choker with a metal heart lock connecting the two sides, along with two keys. "What the…" His eyes move from the collar to me. "You bought a collar."

I nod, my belly flipping again as I shift my weight, feeling giddier than I thought possible. "I did."

He stares at the heart, running his thumb across the soft leather, his beautiful lips parted. "You want me to use this on you?"

"Um, I don't want you to use it on someone else."

He smiles as he leans back, looking surprised. "I'm just…"

"Keep going," I tell him, pushing the box toward him. "There's more."

"I need a minute here," he says, his voice deep and different. "I thought you didn't…"

"This is all for at-home use. As for the club, it's still

a no right now, but I reserve the right to change my mind."

"I don't need the club."

"But you used to like it there," I remind him, holding my hands in my lap, trying to be patient.

He stares at me, his fingers still gliding across the leather of the collar. "That was before."

"Before what?"

"Before you, Rebel."

"We could go together. I'm trying to broaden my sexual horizons."

His eyebrow rises again. "And how are you broadening them?"

"Books and porn."

He jerks his head back a little. "BDSM porn?"

I nod. "Some of it scares me, but then there're others…"

"Like?"

"Like being restrained and being powerless."

"The submissive is never powerless."

"I know." I push the box forward again, but he doesn't bite.

"And, as for the club, I don't know if I could bring you there. I wouldn't want other men or women looking at you."

"Jealous?" I ask him.

"Possessive and protective of what's mine, baby."

My belly flips again, something he's still able to do with a single look or a few simple words, even after all this time. "I like that," I tell him. "But for now, I want to explore this side of me at home, while you unleash that side of you I know you've buried since we met."

"You are enough," he replies, and I know I am. "Our sex life is great."

"It's always good to switch things up, honey."

"It is," he says, setting the collar on his legs before he moves his hands back to the box. "Do you understand what everything in this box is?"

I nod. "I did thorough research. If it's in the box, I want to try it."

His eyes sparkle, and his face lights up. "I'll make all your fantasies come true, baby, but I don't do needles or knife play."

"Well, thank fuck for that," I whisper. "You won't find any of that in the box, but you're seriously torturing me with how slowly you're opening this box."

"Impatient?" he asks, smirking.

"Horny as fuck waiting on you all day. The anticipation is killing me."

He pats the couch next to him. "Come here."

I rise to my feet, moving next to him without hesitation. As soon as I'm on the couch, he takes one hand, pushes apart my knees, and slides his fingers up my legs. His brown eyes locked on mine, his face serious and his eyes hooded. "Are you wet, baby?" he rasps before he reaches my panties and finds them drenched. "So fucking wet. So fucking excited and I haven't even touched you yet."

I suck in a breath, the contact enough to send tingles

throughout my body. "I've been waiting a long time for this box to arrive and to explore this with you."

"Leave your legs open," he commands, staring at me with a need I don't think I've ever seen before. "Don't move them an inch."

I squirm a little, suddenly breathless and wanton, with his hand still between my legs, stroking the outside of my panties.

"Understand, Rebel?"

"Yes," I breathe.

"Good girl," he replies, and the single phrase sends a shiver down my spine. As he retracts his hand, he lifts my skirt, exposing my pink underwear and what I can assume is a very visible wet spot. "No moving."

I nod, trying to control my breathing, which has picked up along with the beat of my heart. This is better than Christmas, and the excitement coursing through my system is something I've never experienced before, not even when I lost my virginity.

He removes each item, carefully placing them on the coffee table before pushing the box onto the floor where I'd been sitting earlier.

Sitting before us is the fantasy I have planned, laid out for him to see. Four cuff restraints, a blindfold, nipple clamps, a butt plug—which, by the way, scares the shit out of me—and a red-tipped riding crop.

"It's a start," he says with a wicked grin on his face.

"There's one more thing, but it wouldn't fit in the box."

"Where is it?"

"In the bedroom," I whisper, my mouth suddenly dry.

He leans over, placing his lips on my neck as his hand slides back between my legs. I don't dare move, keeping my body still, but I allow my head to fall back, giving him complete access to my neck. His mouth doesn't linger long but moves to the top of my breasts as they peek out from my dress. I moan when his fingers press against the outside of my panties, rubbing my wetness against my clit. He pushes the material aside, replacing the coarseness of the cotton with the soft warmth of his fingertips.

I drop my hands to the couch as I brace myself, holding my body upright and avoiding falling back in a pile of horny goo. He circles his two fingers around my clit, causing my eyes to roll back and my breath to hitch.

I feel beautiful, alive, and more turned on than I have in my entire life. The anticipation mixing with the slight tinge of fear is enough to drive me over the edge. But before I have a chance, his fingers and mouth are gone, and I'm left panting and wet.

"You know what's my favorite, baby?" he asks, licking his fingertips.

"What?" I ask, barely able to speak.

"Orgasm denial."

"Orgasm denial?" I repeat, followed by a hard swallow. I should've asked him what he preferred, learning more about him so I knew what to expect.

Orgasm denial. Fuck.

A devilish smirk slides across his beautiful lips. "But

don't worry…when you come, it'll be harder than you ever have before."

I stop breathing, thinking about *the orgasm of all orgasms.* "Okay," I whisper, not trusting my voice to speak any louder.

He grabs the items off the table, holding them in one hand, and takes my hand with the other. "Show me what else you bought."

I clear my throat, hoping my legs don't give out on me when I stand. I'm on the edge, so close to coming from the light touch of his fingertips a few seconds ago and the excitement of the moment. When I stand, miraculously my legs don't crumple underneath me. "In the bedroom," I tell him, letting him pull me away from the couch before he guides me down the hallway.

When he walks in, he stops dead. "You bought that?" he asks, looking from the item to me and then back to the item.

"I did." I smile, my belly flipping and suddenly knotting. "Is it okay?"

He pulls me into the room, his breathing harsher and quicker than before. "Take your clothes off," he demands without hesitation or asking. "Now, Rebel."

Guess he likes the new piece of furniture I purchased, and he needs no explanation of its purpose. I read all the reviews and became fascinated by the idea of being completely at his mercy and becoming an object of his sexual pleasure. The bondage board caught my attention, and no matter what other piece of

EMBER

bedroom furniture for the house I looked at, nothing seemed to compare.

I fumble with the buttons on my dress, my fingers shaking because *fuuuuck*, I'm beyond excited. He drops the items on the bed and pushes my hands away, grasping the material and yanking it over my head like he can't wait another minute to have me naked. When I reach for my panties, he shakes his head, and I drop my arms to my sides.

His mouth is on mine a second later, his tongue diving between my lips, demanding access without asking.

I like this side of Rocco.

No. That's a lie.

I love this side of him.

The part he's hidden and tamped down, thinking it wasn't something I'd enjoy. But there's been nothing he's done to me that hasn't had my toes curling and my body spasming in uncontrollable ecstasy.

With our mouths fused, he glides his fingers down the middle of my body, avoiding my breasts and moving straight to my panties. His fingers dip underneath the material, sliding against my aching clit. I moan at the contact, wanting and needing more.

Orgasm denial, I remind myself, knowing no matter how close I get, he won't allow it to happen. But my body responds anyway. My pussy contracts, my hips sway forward, and my panties grow even damper, feeling the emptiness a little bit more than before.

He pulls back, his fingertip circling my clit, stealing

my breath. "Are you sure about this?" he asks, his eyes dark and heated.

"Yes," I rasp with a shaky voice.

He doesn't stop moving his fingers, making it nearly impossible to think. "We need a safe word. I assume from your reading you know why and when to use it."

I nod. "Mercy."

"Say it whenever you need to, and don't feel bad about it. This is all new to you, but I promise to do my best not to do anything that would cause you to use it."

"Okay," I whisper, trying not to grind my middle against his finger because he's moving them torturously slowly.

"Good, baby," he whispers back, taking his hands away from my body, leaving me unfulfilled. He loops his fingers into the sides of my panties, gently pushing them down my hips, but I don't move. Normally, I'd help, ripping those suckers off, wanting to get to the good stuff sooner rather than later. But this isn't a normal time, and I am now subject to Rocco's speed and his will.

He bends at his knees, one on the floor, sliding the cotton down my legs. When they're finally on the floor, he nudges my calf for me to step out, and I do, standing before him completely naked. He peers up, soaking in my nudity, making me feel more exposed than I ever have in front of him. I close my eyes, trying to avoid his penetrating gaze, and gasp when the warm wetness of his tongue pokes between my legs as his hands clamp down on my thighs, causing my legs to open wider.

He feasts, lavishing my skin with the divinity that is his tongue. The man is a master at oral, pleasing me easily with his mouth almost every single time we are together. Multiple orgasms have been the norm since I met him, and although he is apparently about orgasm denial, I hope tonight will end the same way the others have before.

My body sways, only kept upright by the suction of his mouth and the grip his hands have on me. I moan, craving to be filled and fucked by my husband.

When my hands find his head, he breaks the contact and backs away. I bite my lip, stopping myself from crying out my displeasure, and I hold my breath when he reaches for the restraint cuffs. I stand perfectly still, concentrating on my breathing as he undoes each clasp and secures them on my ankles first. I peer down at him, seeing the wicked gleam of excitement in his eyes, and I know I've made the right decision by wanting to explore this side of me as well as him.

"Wrists," he says.

I quickly extend my arms before he even has a chance to grab the two cuffs from the bed. He smiles, chuckling at my enthusiasm.

The cuffs aren't heavy, but I clearly know they are there even if I haven't been attached to the board yet.

"Face up, baby," he says, rising from the floor in front of me, his eyes lingering on my breasts. "Hands at your sides, feet at each corner. I want access to all of you."

I move a little slower now, kneeling on the bed,

knowing he's looking at my ass, before rolling over and jumping when the cold leather hits my back.

My eyes are locked on him, watching as he attaches the cuffs to the loops lining the board, which provides a million options for restraining the lucky person. There's a smirk on his face the entire time.

"Are you going to get naked?"

He shakes his head. "Not yet. I'm going to play with you for a while first."

I bite my tongue, stopping myself from asking what a while actually means because I don't think he's talking about a few minutes. Pulling at the cuffs, I test their strength, and I can tell immediately there's barely any give. I am completely at his mercy. There for his desire and all that he's willing to give.

A thrill runs through me, my heart racing, my palms sweating as anticipation fills me when he picks up the blindfold from the bed next to me.

"This will heighten your senses," he explains, waiting for me to lift my head.

"I trust you," I tell him as my world is plunged into darkness.

My body moves as the board is dragged and rearranged, but I bite my lip to stop myself from asking him questions.

"I want better access. You're on the end of the bed, but you won't fall off," he reassures me as if he's reading my mind. His palm touches my stomach, the warmth of his skin permeating mine, a directly opposite sensation from the air conditioning blowing overhead.

"I want to be able to touch, taste, and explore every inch of you."

My mouth falls open when his hand slides over my breast, brushing against my nipple. I arch my back, chasing his touch, but it's elusive, moving across my chest to the other nipple.

"From here on out, no talking unless I ask you a question. If you don't like something, tell me. If you want to stop, remember to say 'Mercy.' Understood?"

"Yes," I whisper and lick my lips.

"I'm going to take it easy on you tonight, Rebel. We'll see how it goes, and if you want to explore this side of you and me further, we will. It's better to ease into this sort of thing than to get in over your head."

I nod since it's the only thing I can move besides my toes and fingers.

"Butt plug isn't for today, though. You bought one a size too big, and we need to get one a little smaller, baby. This is about pleasure and not pain," he whispers in my ear, his warm breath skidding across my face.

I swallow, ready for whatever he's going to give me, which I hope includes more than one orgasm. I don't know how much my body can take, but I'm sure I am about to find out.

Carefully, I listen as he moves around the bed, and a drawer opens and closes. My drawer in the nightstand, where I keep my vibrator and a few other small toys, from the sounds of the contents being shifted.

"Have you ever used nipple clamps?" he asks as he walks back toward me.

I shake my head.

"You sure you want to use them now?"

I nod, my belly twisting with excitement.

I brace myself, waiting for the bite of the metal, but I am surprised by the wetness of his lips closing around my nipple before sucking so hard, I feel the sensation between my legs, along with more wetness. His teeth graze the skin, causing me to moan and want more, but just as fast as his mouth found me, it is gone.

"Breathe, baby," he whispers.

I hadn't even realized I'd stopped, waiting for whatever is about to come next.

"Keep breathing," he says before there's coolness against my breast, followed by the delicious pinch of metal against my nipple.

I inhale sharply, unable to squeeze my legs together to quench the ache he's put there. I concentrate on my breathing, trying to slow it as he tightens the first clamp on my nipple until the slight pressure verges on pain.

"You okay?"

I can't find the words to describe exactly what I am, but I'm definitely okay. I nod a response, not trusting my words—and wanting more.

His mouth clamps down on my other nipple, sucking harder than with the first, the mix of the clamp on one and his mouth on the other driving me near the verge of orgasm by itself. Before I can cry out, his lips are gone, and the same cold metal touches my other breast.

"Breathe," he reminds me again, and I do.

My inhale is sharper this time as he places the clamp

around my nipple, tightening it quicker and a little more than the first. I squirm, finding no give in the restraints and nothing to rub against to quell the indescribable ache between my legs.

He brushes his lips against my nipple, causing my body to twitch at the overwhelming sensation. He takes turns, moving his lips and fingers from nipple to nipple, driving me so close to the edge, I'm panting.

As one of his hands slips away, gliding down the middle of my stomach, I lift my bottom, wanting his fingers to work their magic, relieving the throbbing I can no longer ignore.

But instead of a light touch on my clit, he moves his fingers around, totally missing the promised land.

Fucker.

When his fingertips glide over the opening of my pussy, I hold my breath, waiting for the relief of being filled. I'm not disappointed either. I'm dripping wet, the wait for this moment becoming almost unbearable. He pushes one finger inside me, moving excruciatingly slowly and not giving me enough to satisfy my need to be consumed. His fingers retreat as slowly as they entered, the movements methodical and deliciously torturous. He covers my nipple with his mouth again, sending pleasure throughout my body and adding a second finger to my pussy, giving me more of what I want.

He brushes his thumb against my clit, but not enough to get me where I want to go. Just enough to drive me insane with lust, gasping for air, and panting with need.

"Good?" he murmurs against my nipple, leaving me almost speechless.

"Good," I moan.

He moves his fingers faster, fucking my pussy in the most decadent way, and I'm in complete and utter heaven. Orgasm or no orgasm, this is nothing but pleasure. Something I could get used to on a regular basis without complaint.

I already knew Rocco was the man for me, but lying in front of him, strapped down, at his mercy and with him in his element, I finally feel like I'm the woman for him.

This won't be the end of our exploration, but only the beginning. We have a lifetime left in front of us, and I know it will be filled with joy, laughter, and tons of mind-numbing pleasure.

Are you ready for a sexy wild ride?
Carmello Caldo is going to sweep you off your feet.

TAP HERE TO READ SINGE

or visit menofinked.com/singe for more info.

TURN THE PAGE FOR A **SNEAK PEEK!**

BLISS UPDATE

Finish Date: March 17, 2021

Hey Gallo Family.

I started included these little letters, reminding myself of everything that's transpired from start to finish while working on every book.

Las time, while writing Spark, my grandfather had passed away. I wish I had better news and experiences in the months that followed while working on Ember.

But like often happens, life had a way of reminding me once again, I'm in control of nothing.

A year ago, I had three amazing grandparents still walking this planet. But I knew, I fucking knew when the pandemic started sweeping the world, I'd never see them again. I hoped I would be wrong. No one wants to have morbid and sad thoughts.

In December my paternal grandmother passed away

and five days ago, my maternal grandmother passed away too.

I'm suddenly without grandparents. Lost the three remaining ones I had in less than 5 months.

I write the Gallos because I love families. I love big, close families. I always had that too. I grew up in the best possible way, weekends spent surrounded by cousins, grandparents, aunts, and uncles.

And then poof. Grandparents gone.

When my grandma died last week, I realized how small my family has become.

In the last 5 years I've lost my only sibling, my father, my closest cousin (she was also my college roommate), and all three of my grandparents. That doesn't include the countless older aunts and uncles.

Life has kind of sucked at times.

My books don't flow as easily. The words don't come pouring out of me filled with happiness and sunshine.

I'm trying though. I know you're waiting for my words so you can lose yourself in my Gallo world for a little while.

It's my escape too. My fictional world I want to make real. I want the big family dinners again. I want the laughter. I want to happiness. I want to be surrounded by the people I love the most, but will never see again.

If my books aren't coming out as fast as they used to, please be patient with me. I'm trying. I keep going forward because I know I bring joy to you, my dear friend and fellow Gallo lover.

I'll be honest. Ember was a struggle for me to write. I questioned everything about this book. I may have written ten different versions. I lost count at some point.

I hope in the end, you loved Rocco and Rebel's story. Carmello's next and his story is nothing but sexy fun.

May only brighter days be ahead for each of us…

Love Always,

Chelle Bliss
MENOFINKED.COM

Do not go gentle into that good night,
Old age should burn and rave at close of day;
Rage, rage against the dying of the light.

You will be eternally missed.

Millie C. 3/12/21
Salvatore C. 10/16/20
Juanita D. 12/16/20

SINGE SNEAK PEEK

Some people deal with their guilt and grief by getting lost in the bottom of a bottle of booze or pills. I'd never been one to dull the pain without their being some pleasure in it too. There was no pleasure waking up with a hangover or fiending for another fix.

I tried to find my redemption another way.

One full of pleasure instead of numbness.

Women.

But a man cannot find salvation buried deep in pussy.

I tried. Lord knows, I've tried.

All types of pussy, too.

Tight pussy.

Loose pussy.

Easy pussy.

Hard to get pussy.

Nameless pussy.

Faceless pussy.

Pussy in every position.

None of it mattered.

They were all the same.

Each one ended with emptiness.

I couldn't go on this way.

Each year ticked by, no better or no worse than the one before.

I was wasting my life.

It may have been one hell of a ride, but it was still unfulfilling. Every one of my cousins were moving forward, even my twin brother had, while I was stuck somewhere in the past.

"Let me help you," Lily, my cousin, begs, touching my shoulder. "Please. Please. Please let me help you."

She has always been the sweetest one of the family too. She was the most innocent until she hooked up with Jett, the notorious high school playboy that nailed all the tail.

She also gave me the most shit about my whorish ways and made it her personal mission to help me turn my shit around.

"I don't think there's any helping at this point. I'm old, tired, and set in my ways."

"We're going to find you love. You deserve it, Carm." She gives my shoulder a quick squeeze.

I place my hand over hers and peer up. "I don't think I do, Lily. You're sweet. Maybe too sweet and always think the best of people, but not everyone deserves love."

"That's some bullshit. You shut your mouth right now."

I jerk my head back, surprised by the forcefulness of her words. Lily had always been the meek and mild one, but lately, the mouth on her has changed dramatically. "It's shut."

She grabs my hands, holding them on top of my knees. "Look at me."

I turn my head a little because I am looking at her already. "I'm looking."

She gives my fingers a squeeze. "No more easy women. Understand?"

"But they're fun," I argue, getting a glare from her. The same lethal look all Gallo women perfect before they reach eighteen. "Right. No easy chicks," I mutter.

"You want to find your happily ever after, cousin?"

"I'd like to think there's someone out there for me, but really Lily, let's be honest about this."

"Go on." Those words are said with a dip of her chin, moves I know she's picked up from our mothers over the years.

"Who's going to love a man like me?"

She blinks, her eyebrows pulling down. "A man like you?"

"A serial fucker."

Her lips twitch, but she bites back her laughter. "You are a fucker. That much is for sure, but," she moves her stool a little closer until our knees are touching. "that doesn't mean you don't deserve to find happiness. You have a lot of love to give someone."

"I think I have a more trouble to give than I do love."

"You're filled with love, Carm. Filled with it." She lets go of one hand, lifting her fingers to my chest and places her palm over my heart. "It's ready to burst out of you just like every man in this family. We just have to get you to think with this," she presses her palm harder against my chest, "and not that." Her eyes drop to my crotch for only a second, but she made her point.

"That part of me has to be into it too, Lily. It's hard to find one without the other. It may not work that way for women, but for me, it does."

She leans back, her hands moving away from me. "We work the same, dumb dumb. But you never get past your lower half, letting it lead the way."

"So, what do I do?"

"First, we have to find you the right girl."

Are you ready for a sexy wild ride?
Carmello Caldo is going to sweep you off your feet.

Grab your copy by visiting
menofinked.com/singe

ABOUT Chelle Bliss

She's a full-time writer, time-waster extraordinaire, social media addict, coffee fiend, and ex-history teacher.

To learn more about her books, please visit *menofinked.com*.

Join Chelle's newsletter by visiting
menofinked.com/news

Get New Release Text Notifications (US only)
➔ Text **BLISS** to **24587**

Join her **Private Facebook Reader Group** at
facebook.com/groups/blisshangout

Where to Follow Me:

- f facebook.com/authorchellebliss1
- BB bookbub.com/authors/chelle-bliss
- ⃝ instagram.com/authorchellebliss
- 🐦 twitter.com/ChelleBliss1
- g goodreads.com/chellebliss
- a amazon.com/author/chellebliss
- P pinterest.com/chellebliss10

View Chelle's entire collection of books at
menofinked.com/books

ORIGINAL MEN OF INKED SERIES

Join the Gallo siblings as their lives are turned upside down by irresistible chemistry and unexpected love. A sizzling USA Today bestselling series!

Throttle Me - Book 1 (Free Download)

Ambitious Suzy has her life planned out, but everything changes when she meets tattooed bad boy **Joseph Gallo**. Could their one-night stand ever turn into the real thing?

Hook Me - Book 2

Michael Gallo has been working toward his dream of winning a MMA championship, but when he meets a sexy doctor who loathes violence, his plans may get derailed.

Resist Me - Book 3

After growing up with four older brothers, **Izzy Gallo** refuses to be ordered around by anyone. So when hot, bossy James Caldo saves her from trouble, will she be able to give up control?

Uncover Me - Book 4

Roxanne has been part of the dangerous Sun Devils motorcycle club all of her life, while **Thomas Gallo** has been deep undercover for so long, he's forgotten who he truly is. Can they find redemption and save each other?

Without Me - Book 5

Anthony Gallo never thought he'd fall in love, but when he meets the only woman who doesn't fall to her knees in front of him, he's instantly smitten.

Honor Me - Book 6

Joe and Suzy Gallo have everything they ever wanted and are living the American dream. Just when life has evened out, a familiar enemy comes back to haunt them.

Worship Me - Book 7

James Caldo needs to control everything in his life, even his wife. But **Izzy Gallo**'s stubborn and is constantly testing her husband's limits as much as he pushes hers.

MEN OF INKED: HEATWAVE SERIES

The Next Generation

Flame - Book 1

Gigi Gallo's childhood was filled with the roar of a motorcycle and the hum of a tattoo gun. Fresh out of college, she never expected to run into someone tall, dark, and totally sexy from her not-so-innocent past.

Burn - Book 2

Gigi Gallo thought she'd never fall in love, but then he rode into her world covered in ink and wrapped in chaos. Pike Moore never expected his past to follow him into his future, but nothing stays hidden for long.

Wildfire - Book 3

Tamara Gallo knew she was missing something in life. Looking for adventure, she takes off, searching for a hot biker who can deliver more than a good time. But once inside the Disciples, she may get more than she bargained for.

Blaze - Book 4

Lily Gallo has never been a wild child, but when she reconnects with an old friend, someone she's always had a crush on, she's about to change.

Ignite - Book 5

Mammoth Saint is ready to sever ties from the club for good, choosing love over the brotherhood, until someone from his past shows up and threatens his freedom along with their future.

Spark - Book 6

Nick Gallo can't turn his back to a woman in need, but he never expected the Hollywood princess to work her way under his skin and into his heart.

Ember - Book 7

Rocco Caldo does everything he can to not get attached, but when a girl from his past walks back into his life, she maybe the only one to chase his nightmares away.

More Men of Inked Heatwave books to come. Visit **menofinked.com/heatwave** *to learn more.*

MEN OF INKED: SOUTHSIDE SERIES

The Chicago side of the Gallo Family

Maneuver - Book 1

Poor single mother Delilah is suspicious when sexy **Lucio Gallo** offers her and her baby a place to live. But soon the muscular bar owner is working his way into her heart — and into her bed…

Flow - Book 2

The moment **Daphne Gallo** looked into his eyes, she knew she was in trouble. Their fathers were enemies--Chicago crime bosses from rival families. But that didn't stop Leo Conti from pursuing her.

Hook - Book 3

Nothing prepared **Angelo Gallo** for losing his wife. He promised her that he'd love again. Find someone to mend his broken heart. And that seemed impossible, until the day that he walked into Tilly Carter's cupcake shop.

Hustle - Book 4

Vinnie Gallo's the hottest rookie in professional football. He's a smooth-talker, good with his hands, and knows how to score. Nothing will stop Vinnie from getting the girl—not a crazy stalker or the fear he's falling in love.

Love - Book 5

Finding love once is hard, but twice is almost impossible. **Angelo Gallo** had almost given up, but then Tilly Carter walked into his life and the sweet talkin' Southern girl stole his heart forever.

ALFA INVESTIGATIONS SERIES

A sexy, suspenseful Men of Inked Spin-off series…

Sinful Intent - Book 1

Out of the army and back to civilian life, **Morgan DeLuca** takes a job with a private investigation firm. When he meets his first client, one night of passion blurs the line between business and pleasure...

Unlawful Desire - Book 2

Frisco Jones was never lucky in love and had finally given up, diving into his new job at ALFA Investigations. But when a dirty-mouthed temptress crossed his path, he questioned everything.

Wicked Impulse - Book 3

Bear North, ALFA's resident bad boy, had always lived by the friend's code of honor—Never sleep with a buddy's sister, and family was totally off-limits. But that was before **Fran DeLuca**, his best friend's mom, seduced him.

Guilty Sin - Book 5

When a mission puts a woman under **Ret North**'s protection, he and his longtime girlfriend Alese welcome her into their home. What starts out as a friendship rooted in trust ignites into a romance far bigger than any of them expect.

Single Novels

Enshrine

Callie never liked to rely on anyone else for help—until she finds support and passion with the most notorious and dangerous man in town.

Mend

Before senior year, I was forced to move away, leaving behind the only man I ever loved. He promised he'd love me forever. He vowed nothing would tear us apart. He swore he'd wait for me, but Jack lied.

Rebound

After having his heart broken, **Flash** heads to New Orleans to lose himself, but ends up finding so much more!

Acquisition - Takeover 1

Rival CEO Antonio Forte is arrogant, controlling, and sexy as hell. He'll stop at nothing to get control of Lauren's company.The only problem? He's also the one-night stand she can't forget. And Antonio not only wants her company, he wants her as part of the acquisition.

Merger - Takeover 2

Antonio Forte has always put business before pleasure, but ever since he met the gorgeous CEO of Interstellar Corp, he finds himself wanting both. And he's hoping she won't be able to refuse his latest offer.

Top Bottom Switch

Ret North knows exactly who he is—a Dominant male with an insatiable sexual appetite. He's always been a top, searching for his bottom…until a notorious switch catches his eye.

LOVE AT LAST SERIES

Untangle Me - Book 1

Kayden is a bad boy that never played by the rules. **Sophia** has always been the quintessential good girl, living a life filled with disappointment. Everything changes when their lives become intertwined through a chance encounter online.

Kayden the Past - Book 2

Kayden Michaels has a past filled with sex, addiction, and heartache. Needing to get his addictions in check and gain control of his life for the sake of his family, Kayden is forced to confront his past and make amends for the path he's walked.